TOP 8

KATIE FINN

Point

Library of Congress Cataloging-in-Publication Data

Finn, Katie.
Top 8 : a novel / by Katie Finn.
p. cm.
Summary: When popular high school junior Madison's online profile is hacked, it sends her life into turmoil and forces her to reevaluate some important matters as she figures out who did it.
ISBN-13: 978-0-545-05362-4 (alk. paper)
ISBN-10: 0-545-05362-5 (alk. paper)
 [1. Interpersonal relations—Fiction. 2. Friendship—Fiction. 3. High schools—Fiction. 4. Schools—Fiction. 5. Computer hackers—Fiction. 6. Mystery and detective stories.] I. Title. II. Title: Top eight.
PZ7.F4974To 2008
[Fic]—dc22   2008001947

Text design by Steve Scott

12 11 10 9 8 7 6 5 4   9 10 11 12 13/0

Printed in the U.S.A.
First printing, October 2008

FOR AMALIA,
BFF extraordinaire

ACKNOWLEDGMENTS
Many thanks to my own Top 8:
Amalia Ellison, Jane Finn, Aimee Friedman,
Lucas Klauss, Abby McAden, Jason Matson,
Alex Scordelis, and Jessica Shields.

*"My . . . page is all totally
pimped out, got people
begging for my Top 8 spaces."*
— "Weird Al" Yankovic

FRIENDVERSE... *for your galaxy of friends*

Madison MacDonald

is off to the Galápagos for spring break!

Female
16 years old
Putnam, CT
United States

Status: Taken
by Justin

Song: Leaving on a Jet Plane/Lenin
and McCarthy (cover)
Quote: "So long, farewell!" — The Von
Trapp kids

Last login: 3/23

TOP 8:

Justin   **RueRue**   **Bonjour, Lisse!**   **Shy Time**

pizzadude   **JimmynLiz**   **the8rgrrl**   **Vote4Connor!**

1

Madison MacDonald's Blog

Going to the Galápagos for spring break!

Thanx for voting for me for class secretary! I promise I won't let you down!

Join the pledge to get Mr. Underwood to stop wearing the toupee

My brother is a Demon Spawn

About Me

General:
I love plays, traveling, perfect playlists, SweeTarts (not the blue ones. Why are they even in there?), Diet Coke, and my friends. I don't think I've ever taken a long walk on the beach.

Music:
Lenin and McCarthy, Stockholm Syndrome, Call Me Kevin, Tickle-Me Emo, Jason Robert Brown

Movies:
Pride and Prejudice (all versions!), Mean Girls, Clueless, Bring It On, Some Like It Hot, Match Point, Grease 2, Breakfast at Tiffany's

Television:
SATC, Ultimate Home Makeover, Model/Citizen

Books:
Anything Austen, Twilight, Sarah Dessen, Maureen Johnson, Tom Stoppard, V.C. Andrews, Joan Didion

Idols:
My fantastic friends!!! Also, Oprah

Education: High School
Graduated: Not yet

Who's in my Friendverse?
349 friends

Madison's Comments
Displaying 21 of 66

RueRue
You changed your status!! And I see you updated your Top 8 — and put Justin in the number one spot! I guess this means you two lovebirds are official!

Bonjour, Lisse!
Did you know that lovebirds are called "les inséparables" en Français?

Shy Time
Wasn't that a musical?

Shy Time
Oh, les *miserables.* Thanx, Mad. But OMG, congrats!

Bonjour, Lisse!
You're going where? For ALL of spring break?

Shy Time
The what-a-gos?

RueRue
Galápagos Islands
From Wikipedia, the free encyclopedia:
The Galápagos Islands are an archipelago of volcanic islands distributed around the equator, 965 kilometers (about 600 miles) west of continental Ecuador in the Pacific Ocean (0° N 91° W). The group consists of 13 main islands, 6 smaller islands, and 107 rocks and islets.

Bonjour, Lisse!
OMG. That's horrifying. Why are you going there? Pourquoi?

dudeyouregettingame
No, Madison, if there is going to be heat, sand, and multiple airplane rides, I would not recommend bringing your very fragile computer. I can only fix it so many times. Not a good idea, unless you're TRYING to break it. Which actually would explain a lot. — Dell

the8rgrrl
Have a good spring break, Madison. Don't
forget to run your lines for *Dane.* I'm off-book
already. It's an understudy's job . . .

Brian (not Ed) McMahon
Mad, it was awesome that you came to my
party on Saturday. Just don't post any more
pics in your album, okay? I'm kinda in trouble
about it, and I don't need proof on the
interwebs.

Kittson
For the last time, Madison, the prom theme is
NOT going to be "Prom It Like It's Hot." As
prom chairperson, I have to say that your
unwillingness to compromise on a theme has
been very distressing. We're reconvening the
Tuesday after spring break to lock down a
theme. If you can't attend, you're off the
committee. Sorry!

Vote4Connor!
Okay, Madison, I'm conceding the election.
I guess you won. But the recount was
necessary in order to move forward. And I
thought now that we aren't competitors, you
might want to go out sometime. I hadn't realized
you were going out with what's-his-face. So
never mind.

ginger_snap
Hey Mad, I just finished the sketches for your costumes! They're going to look gr8!!

JimmynLiz
Have fun on spring break, Mads! We'll miss you!

JimmynLiz
That was both of us. ☺

pizzadude
Have a rocking SB. It'll be nice not to get any requests for pineapple pizza for a few weeks. ;)

Bonjour, Lisse!
Au revoir, mon amie! Je me souviendrai de toi!

Shy Time
Travel safe! And don't forget that you can't bring anything liquid on the plane or they throw it out or arrest you or something. I'll miss you!

Justin
Have a great trip, Madison. I'll miss you.
— Justin

RueRue
Don't forget: Postcards for your BFF (me).
Sunscreen. Memory cards. Souvenirs for your
BFF. To call me when you get back!

Madison MacDonald logged out
3/23 10:40 A.M.

CHAPTER 1

Song: Coming Home/A New Found Glory
Quote: "Many a trip continues long after movement in
time and space have ceased." — John Steinbeck

"We're home!" my mother announced cheerfully as our
SUV passed the town sign: WELCOME TO PUTNAM, CON-
NECTICUT. SETTLED 1655. HOME OF THE FIGHTING PILGRIMS.

We were still twenty minutes away from our house,
but after two weeks away — two weeks away on a *boat* —
I appreciated the sentiment. We had gone on a family trip
to the Galápagos Islands, in Ecuador, for spring break.

I'll admit, when my parents first told me where
we were going, I had been a little startled. I mean,
Ecuador? For spring break? Who spends spring break
in *Ecuador*? Besides, I mean, the Ecuadorians. Who live
there.

But the islands were amazing — they're completely
uninhabited by people, and were made famous when
Darwin went down there and discovered the thing

8

about the parrots' beaks that made him realize that evolution, you know, existed.

We'd stayed on a small ship with about twenty other people — including a kind-of cute guy my age — sailing to the islands during the day and exploring them, taking lots of pictures of all the animals, and then going back to the boat to have bad food and sleep.

The animals didn't have any fear, so you could get really close to the penguins, sea lions, and tortoises. All that had been pretty cool.

But.

I'd had to spend the trip in close proximity to my thirteen-year-old Demon Spawn brother, Travis, who at the moment was repeatedly kicking my ankle.

"Thank God we're home," I said, kicking him back, as I stared out the window at the spring flowers bursting into bloom all over the hillsides.

"Didn't you have fun, Madison?" my mother asked as she turned around in the passenger seat to look at me. My father took this opportunity to change the radio station from my mother's financial channel back to the sports report.

"Sean!" my mother said, turning around.

"Laura, I have to hear the scores," my father said. "Travis!" he yelled to my brother, who had not lifted his head from his PSP the entire hour-long ride back from JFK. "Write these down, okay?"

"I can't hear you, Dad," Travis said, obviously lying. Because he had to have heard the question, right?

"Well, I have to hear the stock report," my mother said, reaching to change the station back. "Trav, write down how the Dow did today, okay?"

"*Well*," I said loudly to remind my mother that she had in fact asked me a question, "I thought the Galápagos were nice, but —"

"But she missed her *boyfriend*," Travis singsonged. When both my parents turned around to stare at him — causing the driver in the left lane to swerve suddenly — he seemed to realize that his ruse of being temporarily deafened by his headphones had been foiled. "Crud," he muttered.

"Travis, the Dow —"

"The Braves score —"

"I missed my *friends*," I corrected my brother. But as my parents were back to fighting over the radio and not listening to me, I made a face at him and turned back toward the window. I was counting the minutes until we were home . . . where my laptop and cell, my connections to the outside world, waited.

I hadn't been online in two weeks, and I'd had enough of this involuntary Amish-ness. The only internet connection on the ship was through an ancient computer, and they had charged for internet access. A dollar a minute! And this wouldn't have been that bad, except that it took at least five minutes for the stone-age modem to connect in the first place. And since neither of my parents' BlackBerries had worked, I was SOL in terms of the internet.

The Demon Spawn — no offense to my parents — had surprised me by spending most of his free time in the internet room, angering all the businesspeople who actually had important deals to make, while he was probably just playing fantasy baseball. And since Travis had always hoarded his money like Scrooge, I'd been surprised that he'd been willing to spend so much of it on the World's Slowest Internet.

I might have paid to go online, too, if I hadn't had to buy souvenirs for my friends. But the ones I'd picked out were perfect. I'd gotten a bobble-head Charles Darwin for my best friend, Ruth Miller, a *J'Adore Ecuador!* tote for my Francophile friend Lisa Feldman, and a plush Galápagos bird, the blue-footed booby, for my friend Schuyler Watson.

The present that I'd agonized over the most was for Justin Williamson, my boyfriend of seventeen days (not counting the fourteen days of spring break). I'd finally decided on a pair of carved sea tortoises. I figured we'd each take one, since tortoises mate for life. And I just knew that Justin would understand the implications of this, even though we hadn't yet. Mated, that is. Anyway, I was glad I'd bought the souvenirs rather than spending the $60 it would have taken for me to have checked my e-mail.

As my parents finally reached a truce and turned off the radio, we pulled into our long, winding driveway.

"Finally!" Travis yelled, for once echoing my feelings completely.

"Are you carsick, sweetie?" my mother asked.

"Yeah, Trav," I said. "Is oo sickie?"

"No," he muttered. "Just sick of you."

"Likewise," I said, giving him a shove he totally deserved.

"Mom!" the Demon Spawn yelled.

"Kids!" she said as we pulled into the garage. "I certainly hope you'll be better behaved at dinner tomorrow night."

Which was totally random. Like there was something special about tomorrow night? Like we could behave however we wanted at dinner tonight? But my mother was the CFO of Pilgrim Bank, and so a lot of the time she was just out of it, thinking about how the *baht* was doing, or operating on two hours of sleep because she had to get up at 3 A.M. to deal with the Tokyo markets.

"Sure," I said, getting out of the car, grabbing my purse, and heading toward the house. "No problem."

"And don't forget your suitcase," she called as I headed up the steps to the door, where my father had just finished disabling the alarm.

The suitcase could wait. I had to check my voice mail, my Gmail, my school e-mail, and most important of all, my Friendverse profile.

Friendverse was crucial. Friendverse was the new black, according to Lisa. Everyone I knew had been on it since the beginning of the school year. Before that, everyone had been on Facebook, and before *that*, everyone had been on MySpace. I'd heard rumors that the next site was going to be even better than Friendverse, but since it was called Zyzzx, and nobody knew how to pronounce it, not many people were talking about it yet. But for now, Friendverse was a necessity.

Plus, I knew if I stalled long enough, my father would bring my suitcase up for me. He was the head sportswriter for the *Putnam Post* and spent most of his time at home, writing in his office. I knew the sight of my abandoned suitcase would get to him. He saw the home as his domain — or gridiron, as he called it.

It was only in first grade or something that I realized that most other kids' dads weren't home all day, making them peanut-butter-and-banana sandwiches and telling them all about the '34 Giants lineup.

Which was too bad for them, in my opinion. My dad made — and still makes — a mean PB&B.

"Madison, suitcase!" my father yelled at me as I stepped inside, my mother behind me. I heard the phone ring, and my mother hurried to answer it.

"Later, okay?" I said, one foot on the stairs. I had a profile to check!

My father shook his head. "I'll help you carry it, Madison, but I'm not doing it for you."

Damn. That had been my plan.

"And I'd recommend now," he said. "Unless you want your brother going through it . . . again."

That was all I needed to hear. After last year's trip to Spain, I'd left my suitcase in the hall for a little bit — okay, two weeks. But whatever, it had been heavy. And I was just taking out what I needed, to lighten it up enough to carry it upstairs to my room. That was when Travis went through it, stole my bra, and used it in his seventh grade art project, "Ground Control to Major Travis," as the base for the space station or whatever it was supposed to be. And his art teacher hadn't realized that there was a *bra* in his student's project — a stolen bra, at that — and it had gone onto a state festival and won third place.

And of course all of Travis's friends knew that it was my (admittedly somewhat padded) bra that was currently on display in Putnam Middle School's trophy case. This had made me particularly popular whenever I had to pick Travis up after school.

I grabbed my suitcase by the top, and my dad picked up the bottom. I could hear my mom continuing to talk animatedly on the phone in the kitchen, with the low buzz of the stock report in the background.

"Oof," my father said, stumbling under the suitcase's weight. "What's in here? You know we weren't supposed to bring any rocks out of the country."

"Just souvenirs and stuff," I said as we hauled it up, stair by stair.

"Can you believe your mother?" my dad asked as we paused to take a breather. "We just left these people, and she wants to have dinner with them tomorrow night?"

"Yeah," I agreed absently. My thoughts were on my laptop, and how long it would be before I could have my hands on it again.

"I mean, is it too much to ask that we stop hanging out with these people and listening to their interminable golfing stories?"

I had no idea what my dad was talking about, but I really didn't care. The sooner we got the suitcase up to my room, the sooner I could go online, turn my cell on, and reconnect with the outside world again.

"There," my dad said, dragging the suitcase the last few feet, dropping it onto my carpet, and clutching his back. "That probably made my chiropractor very rich."

"Oh," Travis said, appearing in my doorway, looking disappointed. "I didn't realize you would have brought your suitcase up already. I wanted to, um, help."

"Out!" I yelled at him.

"Don't yell at your brother," my dad said absently, doing back-stretching exercises and therefore missing the incredibly rude gesture Travis made at me as he left. Like I was supposed to *let* him continue to use my lingerie in his art projects? Um, no. I don't think so.

As my father hobbled off in search of a heating pad, I closed the door behind him, looked around and smiled. I was home.

It had taken about three years, but I'd finally gotten my room the way I wanted it. This was after many arguments with my mother, who kept wanting her decorator to "do something in neutrals." But I'd prevailed, and now it was perfect. Pink and green, with one whole wall in cork, making it into a huge bulletin board. The room was a little messy, but I could always find what I needed, so I really didn't understand what Gabby, who cleaned for us, was always complaining about.

On my desk were stacks of college catalogs — my mother was pushing for Vassar, and my dad wanted me to go to Michigan, but I had a feeling only because he wanted good seats to home games — and my piles of unfinished homework.

16

There were also towering stacks of paperback mysteries — Agatha Christie, Sherlock Holmes, John D. MacDonald, Dashiell Hammett. My English teacher, Mr. Underwood, had been assigning them all semester, and to my surprise, I'd really gotten into them.

My walls were covered with posters from the productions I'd been in at Putnam High School. There were the normal ones: *The Seagull* (sophomore year, my first lead. I'd gotten the part of Nina after a grueling audition process against Sarah Donner; she'd ended up understudying me), *Wait Until Dark* (last winter, I'd beaten out Sarah for Susy, the lead. Things had gone so disastrously during the last performance that I tried not to think about it too much), *Noises Off!* (this past fall; I'd lost out on Belinda, the part I really wanted, to Sarah, and had ended up playing Brooke, who spends most of the play in her underwear), and *Romeo and Juliet* (sophomore year winter; I'd played Juliet, Sarah had understudied).

Then there were the posters for the yearly musical, which was always an original adaptation: freshman year's *Frankly, Anne . . . The Musical Diary of Anne Frank* and last year's *Willy! Death of a Musical Salesman.* As I spotted my script of this year's production — *Great Dane: The Musical Tragedy of Hamlet* — lying on my bed, I felt suddenly guilty that I'd forgotten to bring it on the trip with me. We were supposed to be off-book when we came back, and I knew that Sarah — who was understudying

17

me again — would be such a pain to deal with if I went up on a line.

My bulletin-wall was covered with pictures of me and my friends: Ruth and me in third grade (the year I moved to Putnam from Boston and we became best friends), then Ruth and I dressed up at this year's Winter Dance. There were pics of me, Schuyler, and Ruth looking bored at the French Appreciation lecture that Lisa had dragged us to last month; Shy and Ruth wearing their MAD FOR MAD FOR SECRETARY buttons from last month's election; Lisa and her boyfriend, Dave Gold, making faces at the camera; the class couple, Jimmy Arnett and Liz Franklin, with their arms around each other (as usual); a series of increasingly crooked shots from my lab partner Brian McMahon's last party; and the front page of the *Putnam Pilgrim* that showed the results of the ridiculous recount that Connor Atkins had demanded when I beat him — twice — for senior class secretary.

On my bedside table, there was a stack of newly developed pictures, the ones taken at the Spring Carnival just before I'd left, all of me and Justin, looking so cute together. And sure, in a lot of the pictures, Justin seemed to be blinking or looking the wrong way, but I didn't care. He still looked completely adorable.

I grabbed my cell from where I'd left it on the bed and turned it on, desperate to call Justin, only to see that the red battery icon was illuminated, and the phone refused to turn on. I groaned, remembering the reason I hadn't brought it with me — in addition to the fact I only would have been able to use it on the rides to and from the airport — I'd forgotten to charge it. I plugged it into my charger and flopped down on my bed.

I pushed aside the pile of clothes I'd rejected during my last-minute packing frenzy, and fired up my laptop. I typed in my password — **madmacdonaldsmac** — gently, as my computer had been acting up a lot just before the trip.

Frank Dell — or Dell, as he preferred to be called. I believe the first time I met him, his actual phrasing was, "I'm Frank Dell. Hold the Frank." Which just sounds weird, if you ask me — had fixed it for me just before the trip. He was the school's resident computer expert, who fixed problem laptops much more cheaply than The Computer Store in town.

And repairing my laptop had apparently become my responsibility ever since I had it customized and painted pink. My mother hadn't been too happy about this; convinced that the paint had somehow damaged the computer, she told me I was on my own with repairs. Travis had offered to loan me the money — at a 21% interest rate — but I preferred to take my chances with Dell. But since he had just gotten it working again, mostly — I still couldn't type the letter Q — I didn't want to make any sudden movements or do anything that might scare it back into the Blue Screen of Death.

I logged onto the internet and pulled up Friendverse. I knew exactly what I was going to see: my page, which I'd just redone before I left, with a really cute striped background; all my information; and my Top 8, ranked in order of importance — Justin, Ruth, Lisa, Schuyler, Dave, Jimmy and Liz, Sarah Donner, and Connor Atkins. I'd actually only put Connor there because it looked good during the campaign, and Sarah there to try and ease tensions between us after the cast list had been posted. But I figured that it had been long enough in both cases, and I made a mental note to move them out.

I couldn't wait to see all my profile views, the new comments I'd gotten, recent buddy invites, and what had been going on on my friends' profiles. I typed in my Friendverse password, which was the same as my regular password plus an exclamation point, and waited to log on.

I stretched and looked around my room, glad to be home. I smiled as I looked at all the pictures of my friends. Life was good.

My login had gone through, so I clicked on my Friendverse profile.

And screamed.

CHAPTER 2

Song: The Best Deceptions/Dashboard Confessional
Quote: "Fine words! I wonder where you stole
them." — Jonathan Swift

I stared in horror at the Friendverse profile in front of me.

I felt like I finally understood the cliché about wanting to pinch yourself to make sure you weren't dreaming. Because although I was looking at the images and words on the screen in front of me, they didn't feel real.

There *had* to be another explanation. This couldn't be happening.

FRIENDVERSE... for your galaxy of friends

madison mcDonald
is sooooooo hunggover!

Female
16 years old
Putnam, CT
United States

Status: Single

Song: Ice, Ice Baby/Vanilla Ice
Quote: "Ain't no party like a puttnam prty!!!" — me

Last login: 4/5

TOP 8:

Vote4connor!

Yannifans4eva!

pizzadude

battlestar, frak yeah!

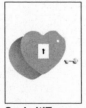

Savin It!Teens

fratguyrobb

Neil Diamond

Addicted to Phonics Alaums

22

madison mcDonald's Blog

<u>omg check out my pix</u>

<u>the inside story on brian mcmahon's last partty</u>

<u>"sailing accidents" and other nose jobs</u>

<u>"single . . . that's how I wanna be!"</u>

<u>suddenly emo</u>

<u>jimmynliz: not as perfect as they seem!!</u>

About Me
;) the stories are true!11!!

General:
hanging with my friend(s)!, macramé, scrapbooking, improving me speling, puppies

Music:
Yanni, Loavesnfishes, Neil Diamond, Britney 4eva!!!!!!!!!!!

Movies:
Dora's Big Adventure, Striptease

Television:
Touched by an Angel, Pimp My Ride

Books:
I dont no how to red

23

Idols:
Billy!!!!!

Goals:
Finish a sudoku

Education: High School
Graduated: Doubtful

Who's in my Friendverse?
11 friends

Madison's Comments
Displaying 18 of 75

 Justin
Hey, Madison. I hope you're having a great time.
Miss you here! — Justin

 RueRue
Hey Mad, I saw you logged in today! There
must be internet on the ship! Drop me a line and
let me know how it's going!!

 the8rgrrl
hope you're memorizing your lines!

 Shy Time
Mad, what's with your pics? They're not, um,
that flattering. I think maybe you've been
spending too much time in the sun or
something.

Bonjour, Lisse!
Okay, that comment you left me was un peu bitchy. RRRAWR! Is the Ecuador Madison just meaner than the Putnam Madison?

JimmynLiz
Mad, how could you put that picture in your album? I thought you agreed to delete it because I was not in the best state of mind when it was taken. Jimmy doesn't understand, and he's really upset. Take it down, okay?

JimmynLiz
That was Liz, BTW.

Justin
Madison, I don't understand the message you wrote me. You want to break up? Why?
— Justin

RueRue
Mad, I deleted your comment. We've been friends for too long to let this — let's just talk when you get back, okay?

Bonjour, Lisse!
WHAT'S WITH THE PICTURE OF YOU AND DAVE ALMOST-KISSING AS YOUR PROFILE PICTURE? WHY ARE YOU GUYS ALMOST-KISSING? THIS IS NOT COOL, MADISON! I MEAN IT!!!

pizzadude

Dude, what are you doing? I can't hear anything out of my right ear, Lisa's been yelling for so long. She's super pissed. And stop writing me those weird flirty comments. We're buds, but that's it, okay Madison?

Shy Time

How could you tell everyone about my nose job — I mean, sailing accident?? Your wrote a BULLETIN, Mad! And a BLOG! And posted pics! This is like the meanest thing anyone has ever done to me!! Delete it, okay?

Brian (not Ed) McMahon

Madison, would you please stop sending out bulletins about my "raging" parties and posting pics? My dad's checking my Friendverse now, and he's starting to ask some very uncomfortable questions.

Kittson

Well. I don't think that kind of language — in someone's comments section — is really appropriate for a member of the prom committee. And I really don't appreciate the sentiment. Your tenure as a member of the committee is now under consideration. How's that for my "supa lame decision making skillz?"

Justin

If you want to break up, fine. You didn't have to tell everyone in a blog how glad you are to be done with me. I get it, okay? It's over. — Justin

Vote4Connor!

Wow Mad, that sounds great. Let's pencil in hooking up when you're back, okay? ;)

JimmynLiz

Okay, Mad, we've been friends for a long time. So what's up with writing about the TOTAL MISTAKE I made at camp last summer that you swore you'd never tell anyone about? Apparently, that didn't include BLOGGING about it. Thanx a lot, Mad. Really.

JimmynLiz

And that was Jimmy. Go to hell.

I blinked. I didn't understand.

I just . . . didn't understand.

Had I somehow logged in to the wrong profile?

I turned my computer off and waited a few seconds. I could feel sweat beginning to form on my neck, and I had a feeling in my stomach like I'd swallowed a bowling ball. I restarted my computer, hoping that I'd somehow imagined the profile that seemed to have my (misspelled) name on it, and that turning my computer off and on —

really, the extent of my computer maintenance skills —
would fix it.

I logged back onto Friendverse and groaned. The profile was still there. And it appeared to be real, not a hal-
lucination brought on by some rare Ecuadorian brain
fever.

But how could this be happening? I never would have
written those things, and I knew how to spell my own
last name.

Plus, I hadn't been online in two weeks. TWO!

I stared at the screen, my eyes burning. I hadn't been
online . . . but someone had.

Someone who had been pretending to be me.

But who would have done this?

I looked at the spelling mistakes, the terrible
music choices, and my friends' angry comments. It had
been someone who clearly was out to hurt me — and
from the looks of it, someone who'd been pretty
successful.

Maybe someone had meant it as a joke? But if that
was the case, clearly nobody had gotten it. Which was
actually bothering me a little bit. I mean, didn't my
friends know me at all? Wouldn't they have known that
I never would have listened to Yanni, let alone *bud-
died* him?

My eyes kept jumping back to Justin's comments
about breaking up, my status as "Single," and the blog

entry. But I didn't want to be single! I wanted to be not broken up with my boyfriend!

"Oh my God," I moaned, still trying to take in the carnage in front of me.

The profile picture was especially bad. I had never seen it before, but it must have been taken at Brian's last party — I recognized the overturned couches that signaled a McMahon party in full swing. My eyes were half-closed, and I was grinning stupidly at the camera while simultaneously looking like I was about to sneeze.

It was the WORST picture of myself that I'd ever seen. And I'd certainly seen some bad ones, especially after Lisa went through her photography stage and was always trying to take "candids," all the while yelling, "I'm not here! Just ignore me! And cheat left. And look unhappy. No, frown. *Frown*. Good!"

This picture was worse than that whole series. Scrolling down so I wouldn't have to look at it, I tried to click on my friends' profiles to see the comments that had been made. But I kept being routed to a screen that told me these profiles were private and I couldn't access them. *Which meant I'd been defriended.*

It looked like I was still friends with Ruth, Schuyler, and Lisa (thankfully), and Connor Atkins (unfortunately). But Ruth's was the only profile I was still Top 8-ed in. That's when it hit me how grave this was. My friends and I took our Top 8s seriously. It had been a big deal when I'd moved Justin to my number one spot, and Lisa and Schuyler hadn't spoken for a week over the fact that Schuyler once had ranked Ruth ahead of Lisa. And the day Lisa had moved Dave to her number one spot was pretty much a major turning point in their relationship.

I tried to access Justin's page again. He had a new profile picture, which was adorable, even though he seemed to be looking a little too far to the left. Next to the picture were the horrible words: *This profile is private. To access this user's profile, you must be one of their friends.*

But I *was* one of his friends! I was his *girl*friend! Well, I had been. I was about to message him to try and explain — my phone was still charging — when my iChat dinged with an invitation from Schuyler. And then she was on my screen, with her arms crossed, glaring at me.

"Shy!" I said. "Omg, I'm glad you're online. Something really strange happened! I logged on to Friendverse, and —"

"You're back?" she interrupted me crisply.

"Yes," I said, "Just now. But I don't —"

"Meet us at Stubbs in twenty minutes," she said, referring to the local coffee chain, and our regular hangout. Schuyler's face was beginning to get blotchy, the way it always did when she was upset and didn't want to show it. We were always telling her to just go ahead and get mad, because we could all tell she was anyway, and at least that way she wouldn't blotch. But apparently, she hadn't taken this advice.

"Shy —" I started to say, but she logged out, and I was left talking to my computer.

Schuyler had seemed mad. I could tell from her face. I scrolled down to her comments, reading how hurt she sounded. True, I *had* promised her that I wouldn't tell anyone about her nose job. But I really hadn't told that many people. Just Ruth and Lisa and maybe a few theater people and possibly a couple of others. But it was a *nose job*, it's not like it wasn't going to be obvious to everyone once they saw it.

And it's not like I *meant* to talk about people behind their backs, or that I meant anything malicious by it. *Pas du tout*, as Lisa might say. It was just a . . . way of relaying information. Getting the word out. A public service, if you will. Kind of like CNN.

Also, it's not like it had never helped anyone. That's how Jimmy and Liz got together, all the way back in fifth grade, as I ran interference and messages and fruit rollups back and forth between them and their groups of friends. And when they'd gone through a rocky patch freshman year, it was precisely me telling Jimmy and Liz what the other person was saying and thinking that got them back together again.

And people didn't really think of me as a gossip. That would have to be Marilee Suarez, the biggest gossip in school, who couldn't keep anything to herself, and was, therefore, the person nobody told anything to. I was different. I was just interested in people's lives. Like Margaret Mead.

Still, I felt horrible that my hacker — whoever they were — had made Schuyler's nose job public. But I'd apologize, and she'd understand that I hadn't had anything to do with it.

Since she'd told me to meet "us" at the coffee shop, I assumed she meant Ruth and Lisa too. Glad for the chance to explain to all of them what had happened — and to get their take on the situation — I grabbed the bag of souvenirs I'd bought for them. If they were all as mad as Schuyler had been, it wouldn't hurt to have presents on hand.

Then I emptied my purse of the stuff I'd needed in the Galápagos — sunscreen, bug spray, passport, pocket guide to Spanish phrases — that I probably wouldn't need at Stubbs. I tossed in lip gloss and grabbed my cell from its charger. It wasn't fully charged yet, but it had enough juice for an emergency call.

I was almost to my door when I realized that I hadn't dealt with my profile. I figured that I didn't have time to delete all the hacked stuff and re-enter my original content, but I could at least prevent the hacker from doing more damage. I brought up my settings and clicked on the CHANGE PASSWORD option. Whoever had hacked me must have been able to guess that my password was **madmacdonaldsmac!** Which I'd thought was pretty obscure, but apparently not enough.

I changed my password to **ih8hackers!!**, my screen name to **Plz ignore the profile, I was hacked!**, and headed downstairs to find my mother in the kitchen, staring fixedly at the stock report on the financial channel.

"Hi Mom," I said softly. Whenever I could get her like this, I jumped at the chance. She tended to get so focused on the fluctuations of the market that I could ask her almost anything and she'd agree. This was how I ended up with permission to inverse pierce my navel, a new cell phone when I'd gotten bored with my other one before the contract had expired, and a one A.M. weekend curfew.

"Mmm," she said, making notes on a piece of paper in front of her.

"I'm going ___ ___or coffee with my friends, but I'll be back in tim___ dinner."

"Mr___," she said again, still concentrating on the ___

"Okay, bye now," I said, backing out of the kitchen quietly. I hurried out the back door and practically tripped over Travis, who was sitting on the steps that led down to the garage, head in his PSP.

"Watch it," I snapped at him as I made my way over to my car, a green Jetta named Judy. Technically, her full name was Judy Jetta-son, but my friends refused to let me refer to my car that way in public, citing the extreme dorkiness of it.

"Anything interesting online?" Travis asked. I looked over at him. He was smirking at me.

"What?" I said. "What are you talking about? I'm going to be late."

"Just wondering if you had any . . . new e-mails or anything. That's all." Then he went back to blowing up zombies or whatever he was doing on his PSP.

Rolling my eyes at my brother, I got into Judy, revved the engine, and headed to Stubbs.

CHAPTER 3

Song: The Perfect Crime #2/The Decemberists
Quote: "Foul whisperings are abroad."
— Shakespeare

As I drove through town, I tried to think about who could have hacked me — and why they would have wanted to. I didn't come up with anyone.

At school, I was friends with a lot of different groups of people — the theater kids, the people in my classes, Brian and his party friends — but I couldn't think of anyone I'd done anything to. I'd heard about other people at school getting hacked, but I didn't think I'd ever heard of a hacking that was this personal. Mostly, it seemed to be Macy's, desperately trying to give out gift cards, or girls named Brandee who wanted everyone to check out their Hot Pixx.

At a stoplight, I realized that in all the profile drama, I hadn't checked my voice mail. I fished around in my purse and grabbed my cell. I loved my phone. It was super cute, as right after I'd gotten it, I had it customized and painted pink — the reason, my mother firmly believed, that it acted a little wonky from time to time.

It looked like I would have enough battery power to call my voice mail. As I turned it on, I looked around for cops. They'd passed a law in Connecticut that stated you weren't allowed to do anything on a cell phone while driving. This had caused Schuyler a great deal of stress, as she kept forgetting about this. But whenever she was talking and driving, if she heard a siren, she would suddenly remember the law and, terrified the cops had spotted her, would throw her phone out the window. She had lost at least three phones this way, and her father had started buying silver Razrs in bulk.

My voice mail icon flashed, and, slouching down in my seat, I called it and heard that I had 43 new voice mails. An hour ago, I would have been really excited to hear this, but now I was pretty sure I knew the reason for all the calls. Sure enough, the first message was from a confused-sounding Liz. I sighed, closed my phone, and pulled into Stubbs.

The Stubbs sign — a grizzled-looking sailor holding a mug of coffee, with a whale's tail arching behind him — was illuminated, and I could see through the coffee shop's plate-glass window my three best friends sitting inside. They were in our usual spot, the one in the corner with a couch, an armchair, and a wooden chair.

Lisa was particularly adept at snagging this spot. She had no shame when it came to getting it. She had been known to spread false information about meter maids, make loud comments about where on the street the couch had been found, and on one occasion I'd just as soon forget, had appropriated a limp.

I stepped into the coffee shop, which was cozy, always just a little bit overheated, and smelled like fresh-roasted beans, and walked over to my friends.

Schuyler, all 5'10" of her, was on the right side of the couch, with her ridiculously long legs folded underneath her. She was playing with her long red hair, a sure sign that she was thinking about something. As usual, she was not wearing clothes that would have made her look like the model her stepmother was always insisting that she could be, but had on jeans and what was probably the loosest shirt Abercrombie sold.

Lisa was sitting next to her, sporting what she liked to call "Montmartre chic" and what Ruth and I called "too much time spent at Anthropologie." She was wearing black capris and a pink-and-white striped T-shirt with little puffed sleeves and black flats. The flats were a new addition; before her passion for all things French had taken hold, Lisa had usually worn four-inch heels in an attempt to hide the fact that she was only 5'1". But as we always pointed out (and which she always pointed out was not helpful), her thick black curly hair added an inch. Or three.

Ruth was perched, with her perfect posture, on the wooden chair. She was adjusting her glasses slightly, the way she always did when she was concentrating. Ruth dressed pretty classically, or, according to Lisa, "yawn-inducingly boringly." She always looked good, but rarely wore anything that would make her stand out in a crowd. Today, she had on jeans — but not skinny. And not high-waisted. Just jeans — and a fitted white T-shirt, with the gold "R" necklace she never took off. Her dark blond hair was back in a ponytail, and she didn't seem to be wearing any makeup, even though I'd dragged her on a Sephora excursion just before I'd left.

And me? I caught my reflection in the window and tucked my hair behind my ears. I didn't flatter myself — I wasn't the cutest girl in school. That would be Kittson Pearson, my nemesis on the junior prom committee, the homecoming princess, and shoo-in for junior prom queen. Nor was I the hottest. That would be Roberta Briggs, who had gotten her first bra in fourth grade — but I looked pretty good.

I had light brown hair, a few freckles, and hazel eyes. I was more flat-chested than I would have preferred, but I had come to terms with it after the jumper craze, when I could wear them really well and Roberta Briggs wouldn't go near one. I read fashion magazines, but I usually modified the trends to what I found comfortable. As soon as it was warm enough, I lived in my flip-flops. I had never jumped on the stiletto bandwagon with Lisa. And at 5'8", I really didn't need the extra inches.

"Hi," I said, coming up to my friends and noticing that even though they might all be angry with me, they had left my spot — the armchair — open for me.

Schuyler glared at me, arms crossed. Lisa pointedly looked the other way. Ruth smiled, and looked like she was about to say something, when Schuyler interrupted her.

"I just want you to know," Schuyler said to me stiffly, "that as of this moment, our friendship is off."

"No, Shy, listen," I started.

"Off!" Schuyler said, beginning to blotch. "Friendship off!"

"Wait," I said. "I can explain —"

"Well, well, well," Lisa said, turning to face me. Then she got the look on her face that she always got when she was trying to think of the French word for something. *"Alors,"* she finally said. "So you think you can *explain*?"

"Guys," Ruth said placatingly, "let's just listen to Madison, okay?"

"She told everyone about my nose job! I mean, sailing accident. In a *bulletin*!" Schuyler said, sticking a lock of hair in her mouth.

"Hair," the rest of us said automatically. Schuyler had gotten us all to try to get her to stop chewing on her hair after she saw a *Dateline* piece on this woman who had to have a twenty-pound ball of hair removed from her stomach. Everyone had thought it was a tumor, but it was actually just her hair.

"Thanks," Schuyler said, taking her hair out of her mouth and sitting on her hands.

"Listen," I said again, only to be interrupted by Lisa.

"Mad," she said, "I can't believe you would do this to me. I mean, you propositioned my boyfriend. In his *comments section*."

"You did?" Schuyler turned to me, looking horrified. "Ew."

"I did?" I asked, feeling the way Schuyler looked. The reach of what this hacker had done was beginning to hit me, and I was starting to feel a little sick. Lisa's boyfriend, Dave Gold, was a nice guy, and I considered him one of my good friends. But . . . no. Ick. It was through no fault of his own, but nevertheless, Dave always smelled like pepperoni.

"I mean, I can see why you'd want to," Lisa continued, straightening her short *Amelie*-style bangs. "He *is* a total studmuffin. But that's no excuse —"

"Guys!" I finally yelled, causing the older couple in the corner, bent over their *Times* crossword, to look over and frown at me. "Just listen," I said, more quietly, crossing over to my armchair, sitting down, and leaning forward. "It wasn't me. My profile was hacked."

Ruth shook her head. "That's what I've been trying to tell you two," she said. "If you would have let me get a word in edgewise."

I felt the bowling ball in my stomach get a little lighter upon hearing these words. "You believe me?" I asked my BFF, feeling incredibly grateful that she was in my corner.

"Of *course*," she said. "Well, at first, I thought it might be you, but after a while it became apparent it wasn't. I mean, you were hitting on *Dave*."

"What!" Lisa said, looking affronted.

"Just . . . that Madison's such a good friend, she'd never do anything like that," Ruth said quickly, giving me a small smile.

"Right," I agreed, giving her a smile back. "I wouldn't. And I *didn't*, Lisa, I swear. I couldn't have! There was barely internet on the ship." This seemed easier than explaining about ancient modems and Travis and fantasy baseball.

"Well . . . *d'accord*," Lisa said, a little huffily, sitting back against the couch.

"Well, I'm still mad," Schuyler said a bit unnecessarily. She was pretty red by this point. "You — or *whoever* —" she added in response to Ruth's look, "told everyone about my nose job. I mean, sailing accident. In a bulletin that went out to ALL your Friendverse friends. Back when you still had some, I mean. Like I really wanted Connor Atkins to know about my nose — I mean, sailing accident?"

"Why Connor Atkins?" Lisa asked, eyebrows raised.

"Seriously," I said, remembering the two recounts he'd put me through.

"No, that was just a — you know —"

"Hypothetical," Ruth said.

"Rhetorical," Lisa said at the same time.

"Crazy?" I supplied.

"Anyway, it was just a what-do-you-call-it. Who cares about Connor Atkins. Not me. But I didn't necessarily want him to know. I mean, I WAS in a sailing accident. What were they going to do, leave my nose broken?"

"Absolutely not," I said. I didn't think Schuyler would appreciate the reminder that once her nose had been broken, her stepmother took the opportunity to call in her plastic surgeon and have him give Schuyler the nose she'd been trying to talk her into for years. And it was just Schuyler's rotten luck that "I got in a sailing accident" was Putnam High code for "I had work done over the break." "And I'm really sorry," I added.

"Well, okay," Schuyler said a bit hesitantly. "If you say you didn't do it, Mad —"

"I didn't," I said. "I promise, Shy."

"Okay," she said again, her normal cheerful look returning. "So welcome back! How was it? You're so tan!"

"Wait *un moment*," Lisa said. "If Mad didn't do it, who did?"

"And why?" I added. "That's what I can't understand."

"So we'll figure it out," Ruth said, grabbing for her purse. She pulled out her small moleskin notebook and took the tiny silver pen out of her wallet. Ruth's solution to almost anything was to make a list. She made them for classes she was considering, movies she wanted to watch, items of her wardrobe that she thought were too similar, and the number of times one girl in her English class said "um."

"Let's get coffee first," I said, incredibly relieved that my friends believed me. "The *ush* all around?" I had a weakness for abbreviations that Dave and Ruth

43

were always making fun of me for. Sure enough, I saw Ruth roll her eyes a little, probably wondering why I couldn't just say "usual." But whatever, it was more fun this way.

Everyone nodded, and I grabbed my wallet and headed up to the counter. Kevin, the cutest counter guy — who was sadly dating Vince the barista and therefore off the market — was working. I gave him the orders for what we were all drinking that month: for Lisa, a café au lait with a shot of sugar-free hazelnut (she insisted on calling it *"noisette"*), a mint mocha Stubsaccino for Schuyler, an iced vanilla latte with an extra shot for me, and a soy latte for Ruth. Ruth was the only one whose order had never changed, as long as we'd been going to Stubbs.

When the drinks were ready, I tipped Kevin and headed back to our corner. The seating arrangements really said a lot about the dynamic of our group. Ruth's chair and my armchair were the closest together. We'd been friends the longest, ever since third grade. We'd become friends with Lisa in seventh grade, and Schuyler in ninth when she'd come to Putnam High from boarding school, an experience she still never referred to except under the influence and even then only in whispered sentences, preferring to call it "The Evil Place." We all had to be very careful not to mention the school's name, and if we ever said the word "choke," had to be sure to emphasize the *k* so she wouldn't think we were saying "Choate."

Maybe since Ruth and I were already best friends — and I know that Lisa had felt a bit left out — she and Schuyler became best friends right away, and thus the group was complete.

"Okay," I said, setting the drinks down and taking my iced latte. "We need to figure this out."

"Ready," Ruth said, pen poised.

"So who could have done it?" Lisa asked, dropping a sugar cube (she'd stopped using sugar grains on the basis that they were too American) into her drink.

I took a restorative sip of my iced latte, closed my eyes, and thought. I tried to remember all the mysteries I'd read recently. One thing that the famous detectives never did was try and figure things out before they had all the information. A line from the last Sherlock Holmes I'd read for Mr. Underwood popped into my head: *"It is a capital mistake to theorize in advance of the facts."*

"Before we figure out suspects," I said, trying to jump-start my brain, which was currently experiencing iced latte brain freeze, "I need to understand how this happened."

"You were hacked," Schuyler told me helpfully.

"Thanks," I said. "But when did it happen? The first time I could check my Friendverse was this afternoon."

45

"I noticed it about two days after spring break started," Lisa said.

"That was the first time I got kind of a weird comment," Schuyler confirmed.

Ruth nodded. "That also was the first time I noticed anything," she said. "But . . ."

"Right," I said. Ruth was one of the least computer-literate people I'd ever met. She only checked her vitals a few times a week, not multiple times a day, like the rest of us. "Okay. So it must have been someone who knew I was away. Because otherwise, I would have noticed the damage immediately."

"Right," agreed Lisa.

"And whoever did it was really out to get me," I said. "For some reason. I mean, they tricked Justin into thinking I broke up with him, they talked about Schuyler's nose job — *sailing accident*," I finished quickly, seeing her look, "and they tried to make everyone think I was hitting on Dave."

"More than that," Lisa said. "I mean, everyone thought you went crazy or something, Mad. *Complètement folle*. The fallout has been extensive."

"What?" I asked, looking around at my friends' grave expressions. "What else? Most everybody defriended me, so I couldn't see what the comments were."

Lisa frowned and pulled out her cell. "Shy, give her the basics," she said, as she fiddled with her phone.

46

"What?" I asked, growing more nervous by the second.

"It's pretty bad," Schuyler said, twirling a lock of hair around her finger.

"Twirling," Ruth said. Schuyler had turned to twirling in an effort to stop chewing her hair, and Ruth and I were trying to get her to stop, as it made her look pretty ditzy. And frankly, Schuyler didn't need any more help in that department.

"Thanks," Schuyler said, sitting on her hands again. "Okay, ready?"

"As I'll ever be," I said, figuring that I had seen the worst of it, and I could handle what was coming.

I was wrong.

As Schuyler told me about the damage the Fake Madison had wreaked, Lisa was accessing Friendverse on her cell phone, trying to find the actual comments that had been made.

It was *really* bad.

Jimmy and Liz, who had been together for six years, except for their tiny rough patch freshman year, had broken up acrimoniously. This was due entirely to the fact that my hacker had written a blog post spilling their secrets.

Jimmy and Liz might be going for Class Couple King and Kween, and present a happy face, butt the reality is something different! Liz and Matthew Reynolds

were all over each other at BMM's last partty! And she didn't confess this hookup to her "soulmate" either! But turnabout is fair "play" right? Just ask Jimmy and his mixed doubles partner at tennis camp, who found love *off* the court . . .

I looked up from Lisa's phone, feeling sick. "God," I said, "this is just terrible. Who would have done this to them? And really, what's with the spelling mistakes?"

"But it's true, right?" Ruth asked me.

I felt a little guilty squirm in my stomach as she said that, but I quickly put it down to too much latte on an empty stomach. The fact was, it *was* true.

Liz had confided in me about her hookup with Matthew, and Jimmy had told me about his fling with his mixed doubles partner. Both of them, separately, had assured me they'd made huge mistakes and had realized the error of their ways, and I had sworn never to tell anyone. And I hadn't told *that* many people. And all the people I'd told had promised that they'd never tell, either.

"Well, yes," I said. "But that doesn't mean it's okay to blog about it. I mean, I never would have done that." I looked around at my friends. "They're really broken up?" Jimmy and Liz were such a unit, it was impossible to imagine them apart.

"*Oui*, they're broken up," Lisa confirmed. "*C'est la vie.*"

"What else?" I asked, steeling myself.

Looking incensed, Schuyler told me that I'd thrown myself at Connor Atkins in his comments section, and Lisa provided the evidence.

Hey Connor, howzit going hottie? ;) I wuz thinking maybe we could get 2gether next weekend and discuss "strategy" . . . want to be my running mate? ;)

"What does that even mean?" I asked, handing Lisa her phone back. "I mean, ew, first of all, but really, what does that even mean?"

"I don't know why someone would want to drag Connor into this," Schuyler said, looking furious. "I mean, whoever this is is just toying with his affections! And he doesn't deserve that!"

"Also, it's gross," Ruth said, looking at me. "I second that ew."

"Kittson Pearson has been really mad at you, too," Lisa said, scrolling on her phone. "But I guess I can understand why." She handed it to me.

Kittson, I think u should use spring break to come up with a GOOD prom theme. You kno, one that might get people to actually GO to the prom, if you havent wrecked it with your supa lame decision making skillz. Think you can do that?

"Oh my God, she's going to kill me," I said, staring down at Lisa's display.

"She's not going to kill you," Ruth assured me.

"She might," I said. "You should never insult the future prom queen. I mean, just look at *Carrie*. And have you seen her nails? She totally could."

I slumped back against my chair. This was awful. Seeing the proof brought the whole thing to a new, terrible level of reality.

Lisa took back her phone and continued scrolling. "I think that might be all I can access," she said. "I mean, I think most people have deleted your comments. Because most of them were *beaucoup* insulting."

"So," Schuyler said hesitantly, "there's also the whole thing with Justin."

I waved that off. "It's not a big deal," I said to my friends, who for some reason looked rather stricken.

"Well, um, it kind of is —" Schuyler started to say.

"No," I said, shaking the ice in my plastic cup. "Because Justin will understand. We have a *connection*."

Justin Williamson and I had met almost entirely by accident. Ruth had been tutoring him in an after-school program, Bunsen Burner Buddies, that pitted advanced science students with students who needed some extra help. I was giving Ruth a ride home that day, because her car was in the shop. My rehearsal had ended early, and I headed to the library to find Ruth. And there he was, looking so cute and broad-shouldered and blond, chewing on his pencil. I normally didn't go for jocky guys, but Justin was special. He played football in the fall and rugby in the spring, and luckily I'd only had to suffer through two rugby games before he asked me out and I could stop pretending I cared about it.

I knew as soon as I finished with my friends, I would call Justin and explain, and everything would be okay again.

"It'll be fine," I assured them. "Justin's not really going to believe that I would break up with him over Friendverse."

"I think he does, Mad," Ruth said slowly, looking sorrowful. "Because he's going out with Kittson Pearson."

CHAPTER 4

Song: Love On the Rocks With No Ice/The Darkness
Quote: "Oh, life is a glorious cycle of song, a medley of
extemporanea; and love is a thing that can never go
wrong; and I am Marie of Romania." — Dorothy Parker

"What?" I stared at Ruth. "I mean, what?"

"*Oui*," Lisa said sorrowfully, with a one-armed shrug that I knew for a fact she had never done before she watched *Chocolat*. "It's true. Apparently, they first hooked up two days after you broke up with him, and yesterday . . ."

"What?" I asked, looking around at my friends. "What happened yesterday?"

"They both changed their profiles to 'Taken,'" Ruth said gravely. "I'm so sorry, Maddie."

Only Ruth was allowed to call me Maddie, and only in very dire circumstances. The use of the nickname would have told me how serious this was, if I'd failed to get it from the whole my-boyfriend-dating-the-future-prom-queen thing.

Because the changing of the profiles was major. Ruth had written a paper in AP Psychology about how the "Taken" status on Friendverse was the modern-day equivalent of "pinning" or "going steady," and she'd gotten an A on it, so it must have been somewhat accurate. At Putnam High, it was the definitive marker of a relationship. The fact that Justin had done this with Kittson was threatening to make my latte come back up. I tried not to think about what *else* they might have done.

So he'd believed it. Justin, my boyfriend of a whole seventeen days, had believed that I had broken up with him on Friendverse, and then without even talking to me about it, had gone off and started dating one of the most popular girls in school.

"I can't believe this!" I cried. "I mean, I bought him tortoises."

My friends all looked at me. "Is that code for some fooling-around thing you guys used to do?" Lisa asked. "Because I really don't want to know about that."

"No," I said. I took the bag of souvenirs out of my purse and dropped it on the table. "Souvenirs."

"Ooh, presents?" Lisa said, grabbing for the bag.

"Yeah," I said, slumping back against my seat again as Lisa pulled out the gifts. "I was going to take one, and I was going to give him one. Because tortoises mate for life."

Everyone stared at me with raised eyebrows.

"We didn't!" I said quickly. "That's a major, major step in a relationship. And plus, we'd only been going out for seventeen days."

I had never done much more than making out with my past boyfriends and party hookups. I had hoped to do a little more with Justin — I'd even bought a really cute lacy bra in anticipation — but now it was apparently completely useless. I hoped I still had the receipt.

"Also," I added, "don't you think I would have told you guys? We tell each other everything."

As I said this, I saw Schuyler suddenly look down at her hands, hiding her face with her hair. As far as I knew, my friends were in the same boat as me — none of them had Done It with anyone yet. Schuyler kept going out with whoever asked her, but then breaking up with them after two weeks, when she realized she actually didn't like them at all.

Ruth had never had a serious boyfriend at Putnam High, but claimed to have had one at her Gifted Students' Science Camp last summer. Schuyler and Lisa and I had endless discussions when Ruth wasn't around about whether this Mystery Science Boy actually existed.

Lisa and Dave had been going out all year, and she'd told us that they were planning to Do It, but that she wanted to wait until Bastille Day, because she liked the symbolism of it. I hadn't asked her what about the symbolism she liked, because I was pretty sure I didn't want to know.

"Ooh, cute! I mean, *mignon!*" Lisa said, holding up her tote bag. "This is for me, right?"

I nodded, and gave the stuffed bird to Schuyler and the Darwin to Ruth.

"Thanks," Schuyler said, smiling, apparently over whatever it was that had been bothering her a second ago.

"Yeah, this is great," Ruth said, bobbling Darwin's head.

I looked sadly down at the carved tortoises. "Now what am I supposed to do with these?"

"Bookends?" Schuyler suggested.

The sight of the two forlorn tortoises suddenly filled me with determination. "No," I said, putting them back in my purse. "I'm still going to give one to Justin."

"Okay," Lisa said. "You mean as a breakup gift or something?"

"No," I said. "As his girlfriend. Because I'm going to get him back."

"Oh," Schuyler said. "Okay." She took a sip of her drink. "But, um, why?"

"It's not that he isn't totally cute, Mad," Lisa said quickly. "Because he is. But honestly, I never really got what you saw in him."

I was happy to see that Ruth looked as affronted as I felt. "We have a *connection*," I repeated. "You guys don't know. But there was something real between us . . ." I sighed. I had really felt this, during our last makeout session. And we hadn't needed to talk about it — in fact, we'd never seemed to need to talk about anything — but that just showed that our understanding was so deep and profound, it went beyond words.

"Oh," Schuyler said. "Okay then."

"So," I said, trying to get my thoughts clear. It had really been an exhausting afternoon. "Let's figure out who could have done this."

"I'm making a list," Ruth said, bending over her notebook.

"Project!" Schuyler said, clapping excitedly.

"So," Lisa said, "it can't be that many people, right? It had to be someone with information."

"Right," Schuyler said, sticking her hair in her mouth.

"Hair," Lisa and I said.

"Thanks," Schuyler said, taking it out of her mouth. "Because somehow they had to know about all the things they wrote, right? Like somehow they found out about my sailing accident."

"You really need to let that go," Lisa told her.

"Someone with information," Ruth repeated, writing furiously in her notebook.

"Also motive," I reminded her. "For whatever reason, someone wanted to break up Jimmy and Liz, and break me and Justin up. Not to mention that they wanted to make everyone think *I'd* done these things."

"I think it was Kittson," Lisa said definitively. *"La femme dangereuse."*

I shook my head. "I can't see her caring enough about me to do this," I said. "Also, she doesn't have enough imagination. Her first idea for our prom theme was 'Prom Night.' And not in the awesome eighties horror movie way."

"Maybe it was Connor!" Ruth said, suddenly, looking up from her notebook. "You know, getting revenge for the whole you-beating-him-twice thing."

"Hmm," I said. "Interesting. And maybe he was messaging himself to throw me off the trail. Which makes it extra creepy, but effective . . ."

"It wasn't him!" Schuyler burst out angrily. We all stared at her. "I mean . . . it just doesn't seem like something he would do. Not that I know. Because I don't. Just . . . you know, a feeling." She blushed, and, muttering something about cleaning up, collected our empty cups and brought them to the trash.

"She's acting *comme une folle*," Lisa observed.

"Seriously," I said, remembering her earlier weirdness.

57

"Done," Ruth said, ripping a page out of her notebook and handing it to me.

The list, written in Ruth's neat, curly handwriting, read:

Mad's Friendverse Hacker/Possibilities:
1.   Kittson Pearson
2.   Connor Atkins

I stared forlornly at the list. "Not that much to go on," I said.

"Don't worry!" Lisa said. "*Ne pas t'inquiete*! I'm sure we'll find lots of other people who don't like you."

"Thanks, Lisa," I said. "Really."

"*De rien*," she told me cheerfully. Then she stretched and looked at her watch. "Oh *mon Dieu*, I should get going."

"Me too," Schuyler said, returning, and glancing down at her most recent replacement phone. "I didn't realize it was so late."

The four of us gathered up our stuff and headed outside. Schuyler climbed into her SUV, Lisa got into her convertible Bug, and they headed away, the sounds of Edith Piaf wafting out from Lisa's car as she drove off.

Ruth and I stood together by our cars, and she gave me a quick hug. "It'll all be okay," she said. "We'll get to the bottom of this. After all, we've got a *list*."

"Right," I said, laughing. "And I'll get Justin back."

"That too."

"You're the best," I said quietly. "Thanks for believing me all along."

"Of course," she said, with an I'm-you're-best-friend-it's-my-job-silly eye roll. "And thanks for my Darwin."

"Talk to you later?" I asked.

"Talk to you soon," she replied.

This, dorky as it was, was our sign-off, whether we were online or in person. When we were in sixth grade, we had thought it was the coolest thing ever, and now we just did it out of habit.

We hugged once again, and then Ruth got into her silver Volvo and pulled away.

I stood for a moment alone in the parking lot, trying to digest everything that had happened that day.

Someone, somewhere out there in Putnam hated me — hated me enough to hurt my friends, hated me enough to try and mess up most of the good things in my life. A sudden gust of wind blew by, and I unlocked my car and got in. The night was still a little bit cool. Spring hadn't totally arrived yet, and I felt myself shiver slightly.

Then I put Judy in gear and headed home.

CHAPTER 5

Song: Scandalous Scholastics/Gym Class Heroes
Quote: "I WAS HACKED!!" — Madison MACDonald

School that Monday was not smiles times. It wasn't like I thought it was going to be a picnic, but it was worse than I'd expected.

And BTW, why is the epitome of fun always a picnic? Whenever I'm on a picnic, I'm usually thinking, *You know, I could be indoors right now.*

The night before, I had tried to do damage control. After my phone charged, I left two messages on Justin's voice mail, explaining the situation, and I returned my profile to what it had been before the hacking. To repair the claims of illiteracy, the Yanni, and the Dora, I added some extra-impressive books, music, and movies; I defriended the creepy people the hacker had added; I sent friend requests to all my former friends; and I blogged about what had happened, so that people would know I didn't have anything to do with it.

I also changed my profile picture, uploading one from the trip. I'd gone through my pictures after dinner and found, to my delight, that I'd managed to get one of Travis picking his nose, which I planned to e-mail to as many of his friends as possible. I also noticed, to my surprise, that the kind-of cute guy — what WAS his name, again? — was in a lot of my pictures. I was also surprised to see just how cute he was. But I didn't look too long because my heart belonged to Justin. Even if he didn't realize it at the moment.

After I'd done all that, I turned in early, exhausted. I was still on Ecuador time, after all. And even though Ecuador time is exactly the same as Connecticut time, I was still tired. The only thing that sounded good was crashing and trying to forget that the day had ever happened.

Things, I told myself as my head hit the pillow, would be better in the morning.

They weren't.

I knew something was up as soon as I parked in the juniors' parking lot and headed inside. Putnam High was big, with almost 2,000 students, square buildings separated by lots of long corridors that often made it impossible to get to class on time, and an acre-big room in the center, where the food court and tables were — the Student Center.

As I approached the back doors, I saw Greta McCallister and Denise Gifford, fellow juniors I was somewhat friendly with, walking in as well.

"Hold the door, Greta?" I called to her, as I was a few steps behind.

WHAM! The door slammed back in my face, and hard. I stood there, stunned for a second as I watched them walking away, Denise turning back to look at me, shaking her head before they continued down the hallway together, talking furiously.

I didn't know either Greta or Denise well enough to know any secrets about them, so I couldn't imagine what the hacker had done to them — or why they would have wanted to. Greta and Denise had never hurt anyone! They played clarinet, for heaven's sakes.

I entered the main corridor with a feeling of trepidation.

As I walked through the halls, I kept fighting the urge to do a face check and make sure there was nothing on it. Because wherever I went, people stared; conversations stopped as I approached and then became louder and more animated as soon as I was out of hearing distance. People I didn't even know were staring at me openly as I passed, a lot of them laughing. I regretted not having carpooled with one of my friends just so I wouldn't have had to walk the hallways alone.

I kept hearing snatches of conversation as I passed: "Madison . . . ," "Said she was hacked," "Friendverse," ". . . yeah, pretty crazy," "Kittson," and "nose job."

As soon as I got to the Student Center, I looked around for Justin, but he didn't seem to be at his usual jock table. But before I could ask one of his friends where I could find him, the bell rang and everyone scattered to class.

My first class of the morning was Marine Bio, and I managed to make it just before the final bell rang. I hurried to the lab table I shared with Brian McMahon and Marilee Suarez, and dropped my purse.

"Hey Brian," I said, sitting down at my spot. "Hey, Marilee. Good spring breaks?"

"Fantastic," Marilee said, filing her nails, eyes darting around the classroom, hunting for potential gossip. Brian simply glared at me, then looked pointedly at the board. I knew from this that he was pissed; Brian hadn't paid attention — without Dr. Daniels yelling at him to do so — all year.

"Brian?" I asked, nudging him slightly on the arm, but his gaze remained fixed ahead.

"I'm not talking to you," he said, still refusing to look at me.

Marilee's head whipped around to us, and she was getting the gleeful hungry look she only got when there was drama brewing.

"Is this about the Friendverse thing?" I asked Brian, trying to lower my voice. "Because I can explain about that —" Before I got the opportunity, however, Dr. Daniels started lecturing us about the starfish we were meant to be dissecting. And as soon as class ended, Brian was out the door before I had a chance to talk to him.

"What was that about?" Marilee asked eagerly.

I realized that the news hadn't spread to her yet, probably because everyone knew she couldn't be trusted. "Nothing," I said, hurrying out into the hall before she could interrogate me further.

I didn't see Justin in the hallways during any of the class breaks, but I did see what looked like several sophomores I didn't think I'd ever spoken to doing an imitation of my face in the bad profile picture.

By the time lunch came around, I was very grumpy, and sick of saying "I was hacked." Rather than repeat it for the eight millionth time, I was considering having it put on a T-shirt.

I gave the Student Center a scan for Justin, but didn't see him anywhere, so gave up and headed to my friends. Ruth, Schuyler, and Lisa were all sitting at our normal table, but as I approached, I gestured towards the school's side entrance. "Guys, can we eat on the rock?" I asked.

The people at the closest tables to ours were already carrying on loud whispered conversations and not-so-discreetly pointing at me.

"Sure," Ruth said with a sympathetic smile.

"Thanks," I said.

Lisa sighed loudly, but began packing up the lunch she'd just arranged on a checked linen napkin. "*D'accord*," she said.

"Good idea," Schuyler said, putting her sushi back in its plastic tray. "I swear to God, everyone is looking at my nose."

"No they aren't," Ruth said soothingly.

"How do you know?" Schuyler said, half-covering it with her hand. "They are!"

"Well, they probably are if you've been doing that," I pointed out, since nobody normal walked around covering their face with their hands.

"I'll text Dave, and let him know where we'll be," said Lisa as we headed out to what had been our outdoor lunch spot since freshman year.

Around the side of the main building, there was a garden we weren't allowed to go near, not unless we wanted to be hauled before Dr. Trent, the Assistant Headmaster, by the overprotective gardeners. But just behind the garden was a large assortment of rocks that they'd pulled out of the ground so they could plant the garden in the first place.

This is because Connecticut is incredibly rocky. There are all these stupid little stone fences everywhere that everyone makes a big deal about, but I'd never gotten the fascination. But rather than clear these rocks away (maybe because they were too big to make fences out of) they'd just been left in a haphazard pattern. The biggest rock, set off to the side by itself, had a nice flat surface, big enough for five people to have lunch on, or tan, or both, with lots of smaller ledges for other friends to join.

It didn't look like the extra room was going to be necessary today, however, as I watched people walking by and either glaring or pointing at me.

"How's it been going?" Ruth asked sympathetically, taking out her peanut butter sandwich and carton of milk after we'd climbed to the top of the rock. Ruth had been eating the same lunch practically every day since elementary school. The only time she went really crazy was with pizza. Whenever we had pizza, we made Ruth get her own pie, since we didn't want any of her toppings migrating.

"Awful," I said, dropping my bag and flopping down next to it. "I haven't gotten a chance to see Justin yet. Greta McCallister slammed a door in my face. Brian's not talking to me, and Marilee noticed, which means that'll be all over the school. Even more than it is already." Then I looked around and realized that in my determination to flee the Student Center as quickly as possible, I'd forgotten to get lunch. "And I have no food."

"Ooh, are you doing a cleanse?" Lisa asked excitedly. "That's a great idea!"

"No, I just forgot to get food," I said. Then what she had said hit me. "And why is that a great idea?"

"No reason," she said, taking a bite of her croque-monsieur. "I just want to do one, but I want someone else to do it first, so they can tell me how bad it is, and I can make an informed decision."

"And you want me to be the person who does it?"

"Well, if you're not eating anyway . . ."

"I am!" I said. "I just forgot." I thought about going back to the Student Center, and somehow couldn't face all the whispers. "I'll just get something from the vending machines."

"I'll go," Ruth said, grabbing her wallet, hopping off the rock and brushing off the seat of her jeans. "What do you want? The *ush*?" Ruth had never understood my predilection for using abbreviations and TLAs (three-letter-acronyms — which itself is a TLA — which I think is so *cool*) and whenever she used one, I knew she was mostly making fun of me.

"Please," I said. I reached for my wallet, but she was already heading inside. I tucked seven dollars into her purse, knowing from nine years' experience that she'd never let me pay her back otherwise.

"Ladies," a voice said. I looked down and saw Dave Gold beginning his climb up the rock. When he had made it to the flat surface, he sat next to Lisa, gave her a quick kiss, then turned to the rest of us. "How's it going?"

"Hey Dave," Schuyler said, covering her nose and scooting over so there would be room for him.

"Hey," I said, feeling my face flush. I couldn't believe that the hacker had hit on Dave — and that he'd *rejected* me. The fake me, but still. "Listen, Dave, Lisa told you what happened, right? How I was hacked, and —"

"A likely story," he said, taking off his glasses to polish them on the bottom of his latest ironic T-shirt. Dave seemed to own the free world's supply of them. The one he was currently wearing had a picture of a piñata on it, and underneath, the words *Yeah, I'd Hit That*. "La Feldman," he said, nudging Lisa, "told me. But really, Mad, I knew you always wanted me. Or, to quote your comment, that you wanted to 'Kwench your thirst for Dave.'"

"I said that?" I asked, horrified. "I mean, they did?"

"Quench with a K," Dave said, pulling a bottle of Coke out of his messenger bag.

"Oh my God," I moaned.

"Meanwhile, I'd just like to find out who this hacker is," he said. "She seems to have quite good taste in men."

"It might be a he," Schuyler reminded him, her mouth full of sushi.

Dave choked on his soda.

"Shy has a point," Lisa said, looking smug. "Still in such a hurry to find them? And stop calling me La Feldman!"

"Where's your lunch, Mad?" Dave asked, clearly eager to change the subject.

"Ruth's getting it," I said, looking around for her.

"Here she comes," Lisa said, pointing, and we all looked toward the doors that opened to the garden area. One was propped open, and I could see Ruth, holding what was hopefully my lunch — I was getting hungry — and talking to Frank Dell.

"Who is that?" Schuyler asked, squinting. Schuyler really needed glasses, but she knew her stepmother wouldn't let her wear them, and would probably make her get laser surgery if she found out she needed them. So instead, Schuyler squinted a lot and made the rest of us read the subtitles to her whenever Lisa dragged us to a French film.

"Frank," I said. "I mean, Dell. You know, the computer guy."

"Is he cute?" Schuyler asked.

"No," Lisa, Dave, and I responded immediately. Lisa and I turned to Dave, our eyebrows raised.

"Just . . . I mean . . ." he sputtered. "It'd be obvious to anyone . . ."

"Ooh!" Lisa said, sitting up straight. "You know, about two months ago, Ruth was always starting these strange conversations with me. She would never get to the point of what she was saying, but she seemed to be trying to tell me something. And *j'ai pensé* that it was about some guy she had a crush on. And maybe it's that guy!"

"Really?" Schuyler squinted harder. "Him?"

"Maybe," I said doubtfully. Dell didn't really seem like Ruth's type, though. He really didn't seem like anyone's type. Melinda Gates's, maybe. "But I think she would have told us, don't you?"

"Maybe not!" Schuyler blurted. I turned to look at her as she stabbed her sushi with a chopstick. "I mean, sometimes people have secrets that they can't tell, and it's not because they don't want to, but they can't, and maybe it's because they feel guilty about something, and —"

"Hey," Ruth said, appearing over the top of the rock and interrupting Schuyler, who immediately stopped talking, and looked down at her hands.

"Shy," I said, trying to catch her eye. "What were you —"

"For you," Ruth said, handing me my usual — a whole-wheat wrap with veggies and Swiss cheese, a Diet

70

Coke, and a bag of salt & vinegar chips. Whenever I liked something, I tended to eat it for about a month straight, at which point I would usually get so sick of it that I'd never want to see it again.

"Thanks," I said, unwrapping the wrap. I looked Schuyler's way again, but she was still looking down. I decided that I'd try and talk to her later.

"David," Ruth said, smiling at Dave and sitting next to me. "Good spring break?"

"Hey Ruth," Lisa said with incredibly false casualness, "who was that you were talking to out there just now?"

To my surprise, Ruth flushed a little. Maybe she *did* like Frank. I mean, Dell. Which . . . okay. I might be able to get my head around it. In time.

"Oh, just Frank," she said. "He and Liz Franklin and I are working on a project for AP Physics."

"That reminds me, I should talk to him," I said, mouth full of salt and vinegar goodness. "I don't think my computer's totally fixed yet."

"He asked how it was holding up," Ruth said.

"It's a WIP," I told her. Four blank faces stared back at me. "Work In Progress," I translated.

"Well, obviously," Dave said. "You do realize, Mad, that when you need to translate all your abbreviations, it actually takes more time than saying the real words?"

Before I could reply, the bell rang, and I remembered what I'd have to go back to. I sighed and packed up the remainder of my lunch.

"It'll be okay," Ruth said as we climbed down. "It'll all blow over in a day or two."

"You think?" I asked.

"Sure," Dave said, swinging Lisa down and around in the way she had demanded he do ever since she saw *An American in Paris*. "A day . . . a month . . . same thing, right?"

"I hate you," I told him as we headed inside.

"Oh, I think my profile says something different," he said as he slung his arm around Lisa's shoulders.

I was telling my friends goodbye and heading toward English when out of the corner of my eye, I saw Justin.

My heart sped up a little bit at the sight of him, so cute and determined-looking, walking down the hallway. I knew I had to talk to him immediately. I had to make him understand what had happened, so that he could dump Kittson and we could get back together.

"Justin," I breathed. "Gotta go," I said quickly, waving at my friends and hustling after him.

"Godspeed, MacDonald!" I heard Dave call after me.

"*Bonne chance*!" Lisa added.

"Wait, who was that?" I heard Schuyler ask.

"Mad, you'll be late for class!" Ruth yelled.

"Talk to you later!" I called.

"Talk to you soon!" I heard her reply, out of habit. I didn't stop to look back, but hurried down the hallway toward Justin.

CHAPTER 6

Song: A Short Reprise For Mary Todd, Who Went Insane, But For Very Good Reasons/Sufjan Stevens
Quote: "If you can't say anything good about someone, sit right here by me." — Alice Roosevelt Longworth

"Justin!" I called, and he stopped halfway down the hallway, turned around and looked at me. I tried to read his expression, but it seemed pretty blank. "Hi," I said, a little breathlessly.

I looked at him, feasting my eyes after two weeks of starvation. He looked just the same, but almost a little better. He had short, blond hair in a crew cut that was crafted into perfect tiny spikes (helped by a lot of gel). He had pale blue eyes and broad shoulders and a dimple that showed up whenever he laughed. Which didn't happen all that often, so it just made it more special when it did.

"Hi Madison," he said. He leaned back against a bank of lockers. "What's up?"

What's up? Like I was just trying to get the history homework from him or something? Even though we'd never had a class together, just parallel PE classes.

But maybe this was Justin's way of coping with his heartbreak, by pretending it wasn't bothering him at all. Unless his way of coping had been to go out with Kittson Pearson. But whatever, it would all be cleared up in a minute.

As the final, You-Better-Move-Quickly-Or-You're-Going-To-Get-A-Detention bell rang, the hallway emptied out. Ruth, as usual, had been right — I was going to be late for class. But I didn't care. I had much more important matters to deal with. It seemed like either Justin also didn't care, or he had an open period, because he didn't seem to be in any hurry to get to class.

"So," I said. I looked at him and tried not to think about how cute he looked, and how I'd really thought that when I saw him again, we'd be talking (well, I'd be talking and he'd be listening) and kissing, and I'd give him his carved tortoise. I didn't think it'd be in the hallway, when I was supposed to be in English class, before I'd really worked out what I wanted to say. But since the other option didn't seem to be presenting itself, I decided to jump right in. "So. Okay," I said, trying not to notice how far away from me he was standing. "About the Friendverse thing —"

"It's okay," he said, shoving his hands in the pockets of his khakis. "I mean, you wanted to break up, so we broke up. No big."

He was doing such a good job of disguising his heartbreak, it was breaking *my* heart a little. "No, that's the thing," I said, taking a step closer to him. "I *didn't* want to break up. It wasn't me that broke up with you. My Friendverse got hacked."

Justin blinked at me, and I smiled at him and waited for the declaration of love and renunciation of future prom queens that was sure to come. But instead, he looked down the hallway and said, "What?"

I tried not to get frustrated. I remembered that it usually took a couple of explanations for Justin to get things. Which was fine. He just liked things to be clear.

"My Friendverse," I said, speaking a little more slowly. "It got hacked. Someone pretended to be me. And then broke up with you. And speaking of," I said, warming to my theme, "I would have thought that you would have at least waited to *talk* to me before you started dating —" I stopped and took a breath. "But whatever. That doesn't matter now. The point is, I didn't want to break up with you. In fact," I said, taking another step closer to him and looking up at him — well, trying to, since we were almost the same height, but slouching a little so that I could look up at him — "I still don't."

"But, um . . ." Justin looked down the hallway again. "But you did break up with me, Madison. Or someone did. So then when Kittson asked me out . . ."

"Wait, *she* asked *you* out?" I couldn't help feeling a little relieved that it hadn't been Justin's idea at all, but Kittson's. But what a hussy! I mean, who asks someone out two days after they've been dumped by their girlfriend on Friendverse? Really.

"Yeah," Justin said. "And since we'd broken up, well . . ."

"But . . ." I said, trying to get my head around what he was saying. "But since it was all a misunderstanding . . ." my voice trailed off.

"I know that now," he said, running a hand through his spiky blond hair and getting it stuck, but just for a second, in the gel. "But I can't stop going out with Kittson just because you got hacked, can I?"

"Yes, you can!" I said, glad we were finally on the same page.

"Madison," he said softly. "I mean . . . if this hadn't happened . . ."

"Yes?" I asked, hanging on his every word.

"Justy!"

I turned in the direction of the voice to see Kittson Pearson sauntering down the hall toward us. She was also wearing jeans and a V-necked T-shirt, but unlike me, she appeared to have an actual C-cup and not just a

Victoria's Secret water bra. As she came closer, I paused to wonder how, on such an incredibly humid day, she had managed to get her blond hair so stick-straight. After watching it for a moment, I concluded that it was probably a wig.

"There you are!" Kittson cooed, walking up to Justin. She stopped when she saw me standing next to him. "Oh. Madison." She looked me up and down. "Don't forget we have a committee meeting tomorrow at four."

I gaped at her, hoping that some incredibly clever retort would come to me. But as I watched her twine her arm through Justin's and smirk at me, all words, clever or otherwise, left my head. "Um," I said, brilliantly.

Ruth had told me that Justin was going out with Kittson. Justin had told me. I had known it, intellectually. But it hadn't sunk in until I saw them together, looking annoyingly well-matched and J. Crew-y and blond, that they were going out. That there was no more Justin and Madison. That it was Justin and Kittson now. I knew it was only a matter of time before they became Jittson.

"So we should go," Kittson said, still wearing her incredibly frustrating smug expression. She tugged on Justin's arm, and, seemingly without protest, he turned and followed her down the hallway, leaving me standing and staring after the two of them.

I had just slung my bag over my shoulder when Justin stopped and turned around. "See you around, Mad," he said, smiling at me. "I'm glad you're back."

I smiled in return, but I didn't know if he saw, because Kittson scowled at him, tossed her hair at me, and continued dragging him down the hall. Frowning at Kittson's back, I pulled out the list Ruth had made for me at Stubbs, found a pen, and added to it.

Mad's Friendverse Hacker/Possibilities:
1. *Kittson Pearson* — I THINK IT WAS HER!!
   Motive: wanted Justin, got him, once
   she got me out of the pic. ☹
2. *Connor Atkins*

Well, Kittson might have Justin now — she might have ensorcelled (SAT prep word) my very sweet, if somewhat naïve, boyfriend into going out with her, but it wouldn't last. Because Justin clearly still had feelings for me. He'd practically said as much. It was only the fact that he was such a gentleman — not wanting to dump Kittson right away because of a misunderstanding — that we weren't already back together.

I stuffed Ruth's list back in my bag and vowed that I would get him back. He was my tortoise, after all.

"MADISON MACDONALD!"

I looked up and saw my English teacher, Mr. Underwood, throw open the door to our English classroom and stride down the hall toward me, toupee flapping.

"Hey Mr. Underwood," I said, trying to come up with an excuse as quickly as I could. Mr. Underwood was a tyrant about punctuality, and if you were late to class, he made you stay in detention for as long as you'd been tardy. The reality of which hadn't seemed important at all when I was talking to Justin, but was now starting to hit me. "I was just, um —"

"Twelve minutes late for class!" he thundered. He headed back to the classroom and I followed quickly in his wake, wishing that he would slow down a little, because at the rate he was going, I was terrified the toupee would fly off, and there would be a horrible moment where we would have to pretend I didn't notice anything while he picked it up off the floor.

"Twelve?" I asked, looking at my watch, thinking of the detention time to come. "I think it's really more like ten. Or eight . . ."

By this point, we'd reached the classroom door with the toupee, happily, albeit precariously, still attached. I noticed an upswing in the whispering the second I entered the classroom, and quickly slid into my seat in the third row, next to Jimmy Arnett. Jimmy's usual happy expression was gone, and he looked drawn and tired.

"Hey," I whispered to him.

Jimmy glared at me with an expression of such loathing that I flinched a little. Then he turned his back on me as far as he could while still being able to see the board.

"Now that Miss MacDonald has deigned to join us," Mr. Underwood said from the front of the classroom, "let's continue our discussion of *Death on the Nile*. So, in this book, we can see how Christie sets up the suspects slowly. When she does this . . ."

I tuned Mr. Underwood out, but trying to look like I was paying attention, I scribbled down random words as I caught them. Motive. Means. Intent. Red herring. Decoy.

Our English class had been concerned about Mr. Underwood's mental-health status all year, but now most of us were just hoping that the fact he had clearly come unhinged would make him an easier grader on the final exams.

We'd heard that Mrs. Underwood had divorced him over the summer, causing his breakdown and botched hair-plug operation. Due to the stress of this, he had apparently been unable to teach us the English litera-ture most juniors learned, like *The Great Gatsby* and *The Ballad of the Sad Café*. Maybe to help ease his own anguish, Mr. Underwood had only been teaching us his favorite books. The entire first semester, we'd done P.G.

Wodehouse, which had been a lot of fun, but probably wasn't going to help me pass English next year. Now we were on to mysteries, and there had been a rumor that we were going to do all the seminal John Grishams before the end of the year.

I kept trying to make eye contact with Jimmy throughout the rest of the class, but he refused to look at me. I felt horrible about the whole breakup — and I just couldn't *understand* it. Clearly, whoever had hacked me had wanted to mess up *my* life. Why also involve Jimmy and Liz?

"So," Mr. Underwood boomed as class was five minutes away from ending, "don't forget to read *The Mousetrap* for Thursday. And I want a five-hundred-word essay on the Holmes-Watson relationship by Monday."

"Mr. Underwood?" Jimmy raised his hand.

"Yes, James?"

"Could we please read a book about an evil, vindictive woman who callously betrays a friend's trust, ruins his chance for happiness, and then dies a gruesome death?"

Mr. Underwood blinked at him, and I felt the gazes of my classmates swing over toward me.

"Well," Mr. Underwood said, adjusting the top of his toupee, "I don't think you read *Hedda Gabler* until next year, so . . ."

As he said that, the bell rang and everyone jumped up, gathering books and papers and heading for the door.

"Do your homework!" Mr. Underwood yelled after them. Then he placed the dreaded yellow slip of paper on my desk, requiring me to show up for twelve minutes of detention after school.

I groaned but simply took it, knowing from experience that he wouldn't reduce the time or change his mind. Plus, I wanted to try and talk to Jimmy before he got too far away.

I caught up to him just outside the classroom door. "Jimmy," I said, standing in front of him and trying to block his path. "It wasn't me, I swear it! My Friendverse was hacked. And —"

"Oh?" Jimmy asked, still glaring at me. "So you're telling me that you never told anyone about me and Anna at tennis camp?"

I felt myself flush. "Well," I said haltingly, "no. I mean, I did tell a couple people. But I never would have blogged about it, I swear —"

"You know what, Madison?" he asked, cutting me off. "I don't want to hear it." He stepped to the side of me and started to walk down the hallway.

"But," I said quickly, following after him, "I'm sure that if you talked to Liz —"

"Liz," Jimmy said, with a slight tremor in his voice, "can go talk to *Matthew Reynolds*." With that, he pushed past me and continued down the hall.

I sighed, hoisted my bag over my shoulder, and headed off to AP History — a class, thankfully, I didn't have with any close friends. So hopefully, I could avoid waves of hatred coming from my classmates for at least one period.

I swung by my locker to pick up my history textbook, and saw Liz Franklin. Our lockers were right next to each other, and our chats in front of them was one of the many reasons I was frequently late to classes. But having lockers so near had been one of the great perks of our friendship — I knew her combo, and she knew mine, and I could grab stuff for her when she needed it, and vice versa. This time, though, when Liz saw me she just frowned and went back to searching for something.

I spun my own combination and glanced over at her. Liz looked distinctly worse for wear. Her eyes were red-rimmed and puffy, and it looked like she hadn't slept in days.

After the reception I'd gotten from Jimmy, I wasn't particularly eager to talk to her, but I did want her to know I hadn't intentionally tried to derail her relationship.

"Liz," I said, before I lost my nerve, "listen. It wasn't me, the profile thing. I got hacked, and someone else blogged that stuff."

Liz turned and glared at me. "I'm so sure, Madison," she said. "You were the only one who knew about my hookup with Matthew."

"I'm so, so sorry," I said. "But, um, Matthew knew, right? So maybe he told someone . . ."

She crossed her arms over her chest. "So you never told anyone about the Matthew hookup?"

I felt my face get hot again. What was with all the third degree today? "Not exactly," I said, looking down at the floor. "But I swear I didn't tell that many people, and I never would have put it on the internet, I promise —"

Liz just shook her head and started rifling through her locker again.

"I know that Jimmy's really sorry about the breakup, Liz . . ." I actually didn't know this for sure, but it certainly seemed like it by the way his voice had sounded when he'd said her name. "I don't think he's doing too well. He seems really upset." I saw her face soften for a moment, but then her angry expression returned.

"Well, if he's so broken up about it, he can just find some tennis-playing *skank* to comfort him!" Liz slammed her locker shut, and a few papers fluttered out of it.

I bent down and picked them up, and I couldn't help noticing they were graded papers from AP Physics and several receipts from Frank Dell for services rendered. I had a similar receipt somewhere in my bedroom.

85

"Did you get your computer fixed?" I asked, handing her back the papers. I was just hoping that she'd start talking about something else, and forget why she was really, really mad at me.

"Yeah," she said, shoving the pages into her bag. "Like, two months ago. And I don't know what he did, but it's acting weirder now than it ever was before." After saying this, Liz seemed to remember that she was pissed, because she glared at me again, turned on her heel and stalked down the hall.

"I'm going to fix this!" I called after her. I didn't know just how yet, but I would. Then the last bell rang, and I realized I was now late for history.

History passed without major incident, except that I had forgotten to do the reading over the break, and therefore was wholly unable to answer a single question about the Hawley-Smoot Tariff. But when in the future was I ever going to need the Hawley-Smoot Tariff (whatever it was)? That's what Google was for.

After Latin, in which I had to decline to decline the verb *duco* because I'd also forgotten to do my reading for that class, I headed to detention, knowing that I was going to be late to *Dane* rehearsal. This production — a musical version of *Hamlet*, set in Denmark, Kansas, in 1928 — was complicated enough to require a lot of rehearsal. Rehearsal I was supposed to be on time for.

And it was extra frustrating, because I just knew that Sarah Donner would use my tardiness as a reason why I didn't deserve to have the lead role of Felia. She had been presenting arguments like this to the director, Mr. Allan, ever since the cast list went up. She'd seemed really upset about losing out on this part — much more so than usual.

I fortified myself with a Diet Coke and headed down to the lower-level classroom where detention was held. I gave my slip to the teacher at the desk and scanned the room for semifriendly or familiar faces, making a mental note to sit, this time, as far away as possible from the arson kid. I spotted Glen Turtell slumped over his desk in the back row, and I slid into the seat next to him.

I'd been kind-of friends with Turtell since fourth grade when he was the short, fat kid who got beat up every day. Since I had a very firm sense of right and wrong back then, and was a foot taller than everyone else, I defended him. I didn't need to do this the next year, when he shot up and became the biggest kid in the class and subsequently started stealing his former tormentors' lunch and money.

We didn't really hang out at all, but we always said hi in the halls and sat together whenever I had detention — because Turtell *always* had detention. Basically, I knew he had my back, which is always a very nice thing to know about someone.

"Hey," I said, nudging him.

He sat up and blinked at me. Turtell was pretty cute, if you looked at him objectively. But he'd always been like a brother to me. That is, a brother I actually liked, not the Demon Spawn I was related to. He had short brown hair and dark brown eyes, and was a nice six feet with broad shoulders. And though I hadn't *seen* any of his tattoos, I'd gotten descriptions of all of them. "Hey Mad," he said. "Sup?"

"Not much," I said, glancing at the clock and beginning the countdown. Since I only had twelve minutes, it seemed futile to go into the hacking saga. "What are you in for?"

He scowled down at his desk. "Nothing," he said.

"Glen," I said, leaning forward on my elbows. "Seriously, hit me. I've got eleven-and-a-half minutes."

"No, really," he said. "I didn't do anything. But people have been reporting locker thefts, so *of course* they blame me."

"That's not fair."

"Tell me about it," he said. "Plus, on top of that, Shauna and I broke up."

"Oh, I'm sorry," I said, trying to make it sound convincing. Since Turtell basically dated the same girl over and over, it was really no surprise it never worked out. But I listened attentively to the story of how Shauna had broken his heart and stolen his Metallica CDs. "Glen,"

88

I said, glancing quickly at the clock — one minute to go — "I think you need to date a different type of girl. A *nice* girl. One who's not going to steal from you. One who's going to be there for you. You know what I mean?"

Turtell blinked at me again, then held my gaze. "Yeah," he said softly. "I think I do know what you mean, Mad —"

"MacDonald?" the teacher at the front of the room called.

"Yes," I said, grabbing my stuff.

"You're done," she said, signing my detention slip.

"Thanks," I said. "Take it easy," I said to Glen, who for some reason was still staring at me. Then I grabbed my slip from the teacher and raced down to the theater for the *Dane* rehearsal I was now thirteen minutes late for.

As soon as I walked into the green room to drop my stuff, Ginger Davis raced up to me, eyes wide. Ginger always did wardrobe and makeup and was one of the sweetest, most even-tempered people I knew. Until she got drunk, that is, on nonalcoholic beer at every cast party.

"Omg Mad," she said in a stage whisper, appropriately enough. "Are you okay? Everyone is saying you had a breakdown or something. Do you think you can still do the show? Because Sarah was saying you probably couldn't —"

"No," I said, trying not to get frustrated with Ginger. Even though she could be a little bit annoying sometimes and *way* too chatty, I couldn't alienate her. She was my closest theater friend.

The theater kids were nice, but they had far too much of a tendency to start breaking into soulful renditions of Jason Robert Brown songs — in public — for me to be super tight with most of them. And I almost never sat at the theater table at lunch, unless I really felt like joining in on a Sondheim medley. Of course, I'd told my friends and Ginger and maybe some other people my real feelings about the theater kids, but I would never tell *them*. They were way too emo to handle it.

"I'm fine," I told Ginger as I dropped my bag in the corner of the green room and fished around for my script. "My Friendverse got hacked, that's all. I didn't write any of that stuff."

"Oh," she said, sitting on the floor next to me. "So did Schuyler Watson really get a nose job? Because I totally thought so, and *everyone's* wondering."

"Um, I'm not sure," I stalled as I flipped through my script, realizing just how many lines I had and how few of them I'd learned. "I'm actually late for my scene, so —"

"Oh that's okay, I think Sarah's handling it," she said cheerfully.

Great. That was what I had been afraid of. "But I —"

"Hi *Ginger*," Mark Rothmann said pointedly as he passed us on his way out the door, not acknowledging me at all.

"What was that about?" I whispered to Ginger as soon as he was out of earshot.

"Well," she said, leaning forward, "you kind of wrote a lot of mean stuff about the theater kids in your Friendverse profile."

"What?" I asked, horrified by how far this hacker's reach had gone.

"Yeah," she said. "You wrote a blog making fun of the whole emo, black-wearing, reading-Chekhov-for-fun thing. You know, the kind of stuff you've told me before. When I saw it on Friendverse, I thought it was kind of strange, but if you were hacked, I guess it makes sense. . . ."

I tuned Ginger out and looked around the green room (which was actually beige). Sure enough, most of the heavily eyelinered eyes, both guys' and girls', were narrowed at me.

"But I didn't write any of that stuff!" I protested. "This whole thing is a misunderstanding!"

"I believe you, Mad," Ginger said. "But do you still think you'll be able to do the show? Because Sarah said —"

"Felia!" the assistant stage manager called, sticking her head in the classroom.

"Here," I said, scrambling to my feet.

"We need you onstage," she said.

"Right," I said, grabbing my script and heading to the blackbox, my head spinning.

This hacker had clearly done their research. Since I didn't really hang out socially with the theater kids, not everyone knew that I was even involved in all the plays. When I'd told Justin on one of our first dates that I was a thespian, he'd misunderstood me and there had been a lot of confusion that didn't get cleared up until our make-out session later that night.

I walked through the lightlock and onstage, where, luckily, my scene hadn't started yet. Sarah Donner, sitting in the front row in her "rehearsal clothes" — overalls and character shoes — with her long brown hair pulled back with a bandanna, narrowed her eyes when she saw me. Clearly, she'd been hoping I wouldn't show at all.

It might have been better if that had happened. My first scene was with Mark Rothmann, who was playing Larry, my brother. And after I'd had to call for line three times, Mr. Allan told me to just hold the book. As I pulled out my script, face red with embarrassment, I saw Sarah smirking, and looking — was I imagining it? — kind of satisfied.

After rehearsal, exhausted and grumpy, I stopped at Stubbs for a quick restorative latte. I wanted nothing more than to take a hot bath and forget about hackers and Friendverse and detention and vindictive under-studies and evil future prom queens.

As I finally pulled into our driveway, I noticed there was a strange SUV in our turnaround. I remembered, as I looked at the car, that my mother had told me something about coming home early. But she really should have known that things didn't fully sink in until I'd had my morning Stubbs latte.

I walked into the house, noticing it was cleaner than usual and that the classical CD that only ever played when we had Company over was on. Also, there didn't seem to be anyone in the kitchen or study.

"Hello?" I called, dropping my bag in the hall. I heard low laughter from the dining room and headed over that way. I pushed open the swinging door, and the conversation stopped.

I stared around the room as my mother said, "And here's Madison — finally — you remember her, of course!"

Sitting at our dining room table were two older people I recognized from the Galápagos trip and, in the seat that was normally mine, the kind-of cute guy.

CHAPTER 7

Song: The Minute I Met You/New Found Glory
Quote: "Unseen, in the background, Fate was quietly slipping the lead into the boxing-glove."
— P.G. Wodehouse

It turned out that the kind-of cute guy had a name: Jonathan. Jonathan Ellis. And that he was more than kind of. Cute, that is.

Also, that it was incredibly difficult to eat chicken paillard when there was a kind-of-more-than-kind-of cute guy sitting next to you, and your Demon Spawn brother kept kicking you under the table.

"Madison?"

I looked up from my plate — I seemed to have less difficulty transferring food from my fork to my mouth as long as I stayed focused on the plate — to see my mother looking at me expectantly.

"Um, what?" I asked, seeing Jonathan look over at me and simultaneously feeling my face get hot. And was it my imagination, or was he smiling? Like, trying-not-to-laugh smiling?

"Mrs. Ellis," my mother said, a definite edge in her voice now, "asked you a question."

"Oh," I said, looking at Mrs. Ellis across the table. Now that I'd been sitting across from them for twenty minutes, I'd remembered the Ellises from the trip — Mrs. Ellis was The Lady Who Always Asked Too Many Questions On Expeditions and Mr. Ellis was The Man Who Always Had Extra Purell. Jonathan, of course, was The Kind-Of Cute Guy Who Was Always Taking Pictures. "Sorry," I said to Mrs. Ellis. "Would you mind repeating it?"

Mrs. Ellis laid her fork across her plate and smiled at me. "I just asked what grade you were in. You're at Putnam High, right?

"Yes," I said, glad this was a question I could answer easily. "I'm finishing up my junior year now."

"Oh," she said, then nodded and picked up her fork. Silence fell at the table.

Feeling the need to pick up some of the conversation slack, I turned to Jonathan, trying not to look at him too directly. "Do you go to Putnam?" I asked, knowing the answer was no. Putnam High was big, but my friends and I had made it our mission to know who the cute guys were.

"Stanwich High," he said, referring to the town one over from Putnam.

"Oh," I said intelligently, "neat."

"I'm a senior," he added.

"That's great!" I said with far too much enthusiasm, and saw him smile that trying-not-to-laugh smile again. Luckily, at that moment Mr. Ellis began talking about the most recent round of golf he'd played, and I saw my father's eyes glaze over before I returned my concentration to my plate.

After the adults had talked golf, the housing market, how amazing the trip had been, how incredible it was that we'd ended up meeting in Ecuador, since we'd never met in Connecticut, and the dollar versus the euro, conversation seemed to die.

"What's for dessert?" Travis asked brattily after the plates had been cleared, tugging at the neck of the polo shirt my mother had clearly forced him into for the dinner.

I saw my mother blanch, but since she was always so composed, she did even this subtly, and I doubt anyone else picked up on it.

She looked over at me, smiling, but with a definite air of desperation, and said, "You know, since we've all just gotten back, I haven't had a chance to restock the treats. Madison, why don't you and Jonathan run out and pick up some ice cream for dessert?"

I could tell from my mother's expression that this wasn't really a request.

Well, at least I could get out of listening to any more golfing stories. But why did she have to include Jonathan in the ice cream run? I glanced sideways, as discreetly as I could, to try and gauge his reaction.

He placed his napkin along the side of his plate and stood up, so he must not have had a huge problem with it. "Sure," he said.

I led the way out of the dining room, grabbing my sweater and my purse where I'd dropped it, and out to my car, which I'd parked slightly haphazardly.

"Nice Jetta," Jonathan said, folding himself into the passenger seat.

I got in as well, and pulled my seat belt on. "Judy," I said automatically, then realized I sounded like an idiot. "The, um, car's name, I mean."

"Judy," he said thoughtfully. "Judy . . . Jetta-son?"

"Right," I said, completely surprised. I looked over at him, and before the automatic lighting dimmed, I got my first close-up glimpse. And up close, he was even cuter. He was tall — and being tall myself, I'd always had a weakness for tall guys — easily 6'3". He had eyes that were either hazel or light brown — the automatic lights had started dimming, and I couldn't get a good look. But he had thick, dark brown hair that curled up a little at the ends and was slightly shaggy. He was dressed in a style that Lisa would have called emo, and at first glance, with his pin-bedecked messenger bag and cream-colored Cons, it seemed to fit. But with his button-down and non-skinny jeans, he put a slightly preppy twist on the emo thing that I found really intriguing.

I glanced away from him quickly, starting the engine and heading down the driveway. *Justin*, I reminded myself.

"Who is this?" Jonathan asked, and I was jerked out of my reveries to see him frowning at my iCar.

"Um, Stockholm Syndrome," I said, turning the volume down slightly. He continued to frown, and I raised my eyebrows. "Do you have something against Swedish guitar bands, Jonathan?"

"Nathan," he said firmly. "Well, really, everyone calls me Nate. Only my parents call me Jonathan."

"Nate," I said, trying it out. I liked it. It seemed to fit him better, somehow. "Nate the Great, right?"

"Yeah," he said with a small sigh. I got the feeling he'd heard that before.

"Nate the Great," I said, trying to remember, "the boy detective."

"That was Encyclopedia Brown," he said. "But close enough."

"Right." I was beginning to worry about the next song that was going to come up on my shuffle setting. If he had a problem with Stockholm Syndrome — which was some of the cooler music on my iCar — I could only imagine what he'd think about my Kelly Clarkson.

"So is it just Madison?" he asked.

"Yes," I said. "I mean, my friends call me Mad or Mads."

"Got it."

"I mean, they used to," I said after a moment of silence, punctuated only by Olaf's soulful wailing. "Back when I had friends, that is."

We pulled up to Gofer Ice Cream, which was in the same complex as Putnam Pizza, where Dave worked. I scanned the parking lot, but didn't see his car parked anywhere, so I figured he must not have been working. The song changed just as I put the car into park.

"Is this Kelly Clarkson?" Nate asked incredulously.

"Um, no," I said as I killed the engine quickly. I got out, locked the car, and headed into Gofer just behind Nate, trying not to notice how cute his butt looked in his dark-wash jeans.

I picked up what my mother usually kept on hand — pints of vanilla and chocolate ice cream, and raspberry and lemon sorbets. And for the ride home, I got a cone of hazelnut gelato. To my surprise, Nate ordered himself a cone of mint chocolate chip. It wasn't until I walked out of the store that I realized I should have ordered a cup. It was going to be impossible to drive and eat my gelato at the same time.

I suddenly felt like an idiot. Ruth, no doubt, would have foreseen this and ordered a cup. Actually, she probably wouldn't have gotten anything for herself and would have brought the ice cream directly home for the hungry people who wanted dessert. But whatever.

There was a little patio just outside the store, with benches and chairs. I gestured to it. "Mind if we sit for a moment? I don't think I'm going to be able to handle this cone while driving."

"Sure," Nate said, and we sat down next to each other — but not too close — on the bench. "What did you mean?" he asked after a moment of silent ice cream consumption. "That thing with your friends?"

"What thing?" I asked, my mouth full of gelato-y goodness.

"You said that your friends used to call you by your nickname — back when you had friends." He took a bite, eyebrows raised. "Care to explicate?"

"Oh," I said, trying not to swoon at the SAT vocab word usage, "that. It's kind of a long story."

"It's kind of a big cone," he said, gesturing to his quickly melting mint chocolate chip.

"Well," I said, thinking. I was a little bit nervous about sharing this much of my life with someone who was pretty much a stranger. And a lot of the details were pretty embarrassing for me. But I did want to talk about it, and with someone who wasn't involved at all. And there was just something about Nate that made me think I could trust him. "Okay." I took a bite of gelato for strength and launched into the whole Friendversegate saga.

"And," I concluded a few minutes later, trying desperately to stem the flow of my melting gelato with napkins. I hadn't had much time to eat during the story — because I'd been talking — and my cone was overflowing. Nate, on the other hand, was practically done with his mint chocolate chip, and at this point was just eating the waffle cone. "That's about it. So, to make a long story short —"

"Too late," Nate interrupted.

"Excuse me?" I asked, offended, as I drank some of my gelato.

"No," he said quickly, perhaps noticing my expression, "I was just quoting. It's from *Clue*."

"The board game?"

"No, the movie."

"They made a movie about the board game? What, is it like a documentary of people playing it or something?" I took another drink.

"No," he said again, a little more serious-sounding this time, "it's a classic comedy. Pretty much required watching, in my opinion." He finished his last bite of waffle cone and brushed his hands off. "I'm surprised you haven't heard of it. You should check it out."

"Maybe," I said a little huffily. I mean, just because I hadn't heard of some obscure movie, there was no need to make me seem like an uncultured idiot. Justin had never recommended movies to me.

Well, that might have been because Justin had only seemed to like movies in which there was an explosion every five minutes and girls who got naked for reasons that always seemed to defy logic.

"So anyway, that's the story," I said, trying to figure out what to do with my gelato-soaked napkins.

Nate didn't say anything for a moment, but he did take my napkins from me and threw them out in the trash that was right next to him. "I just don't get why it's such a big deal," he finally said. "The whole hacking thing, that is."

I stared at him. Maybe I'd used too many small words, and hadn't *explicated* properly. "It's a big deal," I said slowly, "because my life is over. Because I'm now held responsible for my friends' breakup. Because everyone hates me. Because my identity was stolen, and by some-one who can't spell my last name correctly."

"Your profile was hacked," he said. "It really doesn't have anything to do with you or who you are."

Had he not understood the story? It seemed like he'd been paying attention; he'd been looking at me pretty intently, after all. "It has everything to do with who I am. That profile was my life!"

Nate shook his head and leaned back against the bench. "It isn't your life," he said. "It's your online list of bands you like and pictures of you and your friends."

"It's more than that," I said, hearing my voice rise slightly. "My boyfriend broke up with me because of that profile. Or, that is, he believed that I broke up with him. And as a result is now dating the soon-to-be prom queen. But that's another story."

"If he allowed himself to be broken up with over Friendverse, without talking to you about it first, you're probably better off without him."

I just shook my head. Nate was only saying that because he had no idea what a great kisser Justin was or how good he looked with his shirt off — facts I was actually pretty glad he wasn't privy to. "You just don't get it," I said, finishing off the gelato soup and starting in on the cone.

"I don't," he agreed, leaning a little closer to me and looking at me intently.

And I'll admit it, my heart gave a little excited *thump*, the kind it hadn't given since Justin and I first started making — I mean, going — out. I noticed in the fluorescent light of the bug zapper that Nate's eyes were a light, amber-y brown. And that he smelled good, not of cologne like Justin, but of boy-soap and cinnamon gum and mint chocolate chip.

"I have a Friendverse profile," he continued, "but it's not my life. I only check it about twice a week. And if I'd been hacked, my friends would have thought it was a huge joke. They wouldn't have believed it."

"Well, not everybody believed it," I said slowly. "My best friend believed me. And after I told my two other best friends it wasn't true, they believed me too."

"Maybe that should tell you something," he said. He held my gaze for just a moment longer, and my heart started beating triple-time. But that was probably just because of the sugar.

"We should probably get back," I said, breaking our eye contact and looking down at my *Gofer To Go . . . fer!* plastic bag. "The ice cream's going to melt."

"Right," he said. He followed me out to the car and I unlocked it. Before he got in, though, he turned back to Gofer and pulled a small camera out of his pocket. He held it up and pointed it toward the large blink-ing ice cream cone just outside the store. He took a cou-ple of shots, then closed his camera and looked over at me.

"What was that?" I asked.

Nate shrugged, holding his camera, looking a little embarrassed for the first time that night. "I don't know," he said. "I guess I just have a weakness for things that are beautiful."

Then he got in the passenger seat, leaving me staring at the neon ice cream cone blinking against the darkening sky, wondering what was beautiful about it.

Giving up, I got in. When I turned the car on, he cranked the stereo up and pointed to the small glowing screen of the iCar. "I knew it!" he said, laughing. "Kelly Clarkson."

Later, after we'd gotten back and I'd blamed the delay on late-night traffic and said goodbye to the Ellises and helped Dad with the dishes and added *Clue* to my Netflix queue, I checked my Friendverse.

Madison's Inbox
Buddy Invites: 1 New
North by NE/Nate Ellis wants to be your friend!

FRIENDVERSE... for your galaxy of friends

North by NE
has a sugar high

Male
18 years old
Stanwich, CT
United States

Status: Single

Song: Jenny & the Ess-Dog/Stephen Malkmus
Quote: "I hate quotations. Tell me what you know." — Emerson

Last login: 4/7

TOP 8:

evan

em-squared

they call me mr. gibbs

Brian (not Ed) McMahon

Melissa

Casey! At the Disco

Dani/California

nickVerse

North by NE's blog

ice cream

Pulling a Charlie D, going to the Galápagos

Harboring a few emo thoughts

breakups suck

About Me

General:
Lee, Hospital, Admission, Electric

Music:
MU-330, Pop Girls Etc, Pavlov's Dog, Fruitless Gourd, Johnny Cash, Bob Dylan

Movies:
Terrence Malick, Robert Altman, Noah Baumbach, Wes Anderson, Whit Stillman, Woody Allen, Francois Truffaut, Serge Gainsbourg, Billy Wilder, Alfred Hitchcock

Television:
I don't watch TV.

Books:
Bukowski, Wodehouse, Carver, Whitman, Gorevitch, Didion, Sedaris

Idols:
Graven

Education: High School
Graduated: In 2 months . . .

Who's in my Friendverse?
185 friends

North by NE's Comments
Displaying 6 of 55

evan
Dude, glad you're back. Let's hit Stanwich
Sandwich for a BLT stat.

they call me mr. gibbs
sweet profile song. Can I get my CD back one
of these days?

em-squared
Hey hon, I missed you! How was Peru? Call me!

Brian (not Ed) McMahon
dude, you have no idea. He melted down. It
was like Three Mile Island at my house. I'll call
you when I'm allowed out again — maybe in
10 years?

Melissa
Went by our place the other day & thought
about you. how've you been?

nickVerse
you went WHERE for spring break?

CHAPTER 8

Song: Suspect Fled The Scene/Pedro the Lion
Quote: "The game is afoot!" — Sherlock Holmes

"So how was it?" Schuyler asked as she stood in front of her locker. It was Tuesday morning, and I had an open period, so I could stand with her and discuss Nate's profile while she struggled to remember her combination. This was not a rare occurrence. Schuyler forgot her combination about once a week. She'd started writing it down, but then she usually forgot what she did with the paper.

I leaned against the locker next to hers. I'd certainly spent enough time staring at the profile last night, and describing it over the phone to Ruth and Lisa. (We figured it would be too suspicious for people who were in my Top 8 to suddenly be friending him.) Ruth had seemed impressed, but Lisa hadn't been that much help in analysis, because as soon as she heard about the references to Truffaut and Gainsbourg, she'd decided he had good taste, and had hung up so she could add them to her own profile.

I was more interested than I thought I'd be to see that his status was "Single." And that we had some writers and directors in common. Mostly, though, his prof seemed really intimidating. And it was a little weird to think about the fact that, after I'd accepted his buddy invite, he could now see *my* profile as well. I was really wondering what he thought about it, for some reason.

And I couldn't help getting a little fluttery feeling in my stomach when I thought about him looking for me on Friendverse.

But the thing that was giving me the most food for thought was his most recent blog entry, entitled "ice cream." It must have been posted right after he'd gotten back from our house. It simply said:

it's always when you
are not looking that you get
a treat. mint choc chip.

It had taken me a little longer than it should have (don't tell last year's English teacher) to realize this wasn't just a weirdly formatted blog, but a haiku. I figured that it was probably just about what the title said: ice cream. But I'd still looked at it for much longer than it takes to read seventeen syllables.

"Mad?" Schuyler prompted.

"Sorry," I said, pulled out of my own thoughts. "It was good," I said. "Just a little . . . intimidating. I don't know. He seems really smart and is into weird bands I've never heard of."

"But you're smart, Mad," Schuyler said. "And you like weird bands too!" she added encouragingly. "But, um, what about Justin?"

"What do you mean?"

"I mean," she said, twirling the dial again, "are you still going to try and get him back or have you moved on to this cute senior guy? Or, um, someone else?"

"His name is Nate," I reminded her. "And of course I'm going to try and get Justin back! I'm going to show him that we belong together." As soon as I said this, though, I felt a tiny twinge of doubt. *Did* we still belong together? But I quickly pushed the thought away. *Tortoise*, I reminded myself. "And who else would we be talking about?" I asked, genuinely puzzled.

Schuyler seemed not to hear me, as she stopped twirling and stared bleakly at her locker. "I think I'm going to have to go to the office again."

"I'll walk with." We headed down the corridor together. People were still pointing and whispering as I passed, but it was a little less pronounced than it had been the day before. This might have had something to do with the fact that Jimmy — whose new

Friendverse name was **Liz is a whore** — and Liz — whose name had changed to **Jimmy has a teeny tiny** . . . — had sent out multiple bulletins about each other, giving me much more information than I'd ever wanted to know about their relationship and certain parts of Jimmy's anatomy.

The office was deserted, except for Glen Turtell, who was sitting in his usual spot outside Assistant Headmaster Trent's office. Turtell greeted us with a "Sup," looked at me for maybe a moment longer than usual, then went back to carving his name into the bench, which was one of the stupider things I'd ever seen him do, since he was practically confessing to the crime as he was committing it.

Stephanie, Dr. Trent's secretary, was manning the desk. She sighed when she saw Schuyler. "Combination again?"

"Yes," Schuyler said meekly. "Sorry."

"I thought I told you to write it down," Stephanie said.

"I did," Schuyler protested. "You told me to, Madison here told me to, and I *did*, I just can't find the piece of paper."

Stephanie looked at me with interest. "You're Madison?" she asked.

"And then I put it in my phone," Schuyler continued, seemingly unaware the conversation had gone on. "But then I threw it out the window —"

112

"Madison MacDonald?" Stephanie asked.

"Um, yes," I said, beginning to get nervous. Unlike Schuyler and Turtell, I was almost never in the office, and I preferred to keep it that way.

"Just a second, Miss Watson," Stephanie said to Schuyler. "All the locker combinations have been stored in a secure database on Dr. Trent's computer. We've had some problems with locker thefts." As she said this, she glared at Turtell, who frowned right back. "Don't go any-where, Madison," she added to me as she disappeared into Dr. Trent's office.

Schuyler turned to me, eyes wide. "What'd you do?"

"Run for it, dude," Turtell advised. "Don't look back."

"I didn't do anything," I said, wracking my brain for any violation of school policies I may have accidentally committed. But then I realized it probably was some-thing to do with student government. Due to Connor Atkins's recount issues, I hadn't been at the initial meet-ing with the other officers. Dr. Trent just probably wanted to welcome me formally or something.

"Here you go," Stephanie said, returning and hand-ing Schuyler a piece of paper. "Please keep track of it this time."

"I will," Schuyler promised. I saw her eyes dart up to the clock above Stephanie's desk. "Um, is there any way you could write me a pass for class?"

"Shy," I said quickly, hoping to get some info before she had to leave, "what did you mean before —"

"Madison MacDonald!" Dr. Trent stuck his head out of his office and motioned at me. "Would you mind coming in here, please?" He pointed at Turtell. "I'll deal with you in a moment, young man."

"But I was here first!" Turtell protested.

"Madison," Dr. Trent said again, and disappeared into his office.

I waved goodbye to Schuyler and followed. I'd only been in Dr. Trent's office one other time, due to a misunderstanding freshman year when I'd been assigned Boys' PE (stupid gender-neutral name) and refused, for obvious reasons, to go. Little seemed to have changed in two years; it was still stark and intimidating. However, there were now several framed inspirational posters of soaring eagles that said things like *Why run when you can fly?*

Which didn't really make any sense to me at all. Unless it was an inspirational poster for actual eagles.

I took the seat in front of the desk and looked across at Dr. Trent, who steepled his fingers and frowned at me.

"I have an open," I said, to fill the silence. "I'm not cutting or anything."

"Miss MacDonald," he said, pulling a file out from under his desk, "I'm afraid that a certain . . . matter has come to my attention."

"Okay," I said, beginning to doubt that he was now going to welcome me warmly into the PHS student government family.

He opened the file and I saw, to my horror, a printout of my hacked profile, in all its misspelled glory.

"How . . . how did you get that?" I choked out.

"You're aware, of course, that all Putnam High students belonging to this social networking site have to 'buddy' the profile of Putnam High School?"

Faint, faint bells were ringing from when I joined Friendverse. I remembered getting the bulletin from the school, which stated that all students had to approve the invite from the incredibly lame PHS profile. Apparently, it was to prevent students cheating and posting tests. But I hadn't been doing anything like that.

"Yes," I replied slowly.

"Well," Dr. Trent said, flipping through the pages of my profile, "your particular profile has recently been . . . brought to my attention."

"Wait," I said quickly. "My profile was hacked while I was away on spring break. I didn't write any of that stuff." Inwardly I sighed, wondering how many more times I would be required to say that sentence. "If you check it now, you'll see it's all been restored."

"Hmm," he said, making a note on the file. "I'll look into that. But this is troubling," he said, looking over the tops of his glasses at me. "Quite troubling."

"I agree!" I agreed. "I mean, I don't even know how someone managed to hack my profile in the first place!" As I said this, I realized that I'd failed to ask myself that very question. How *had* someone managed to hack into my profile?

"Well," he said, closing the file, "I'll continue to monitor the situation. But as Mr. Atkins pointed out, Miss MacDonald, this" — he held up the file for emphasis — "is not the kind of thing we expect from our student government officers."

I had been in the process of getting my stuff together, but I stopped and sat straight up. "Mr. Atkins?" I asked. "*Connor* Atkins? He's the one who told you about this?"

"I don't know if I'm at liberty to disclose that," Dr. Trent said stiffly, as he placed my file in his drawer. "But he did point out — and I quite agree — that our student officers need to represent the best parts of Putnam High School, and —"

"Naturally," I said, inwardly seething. "But as I've told you before, I had nothing to do with this. My *profile* was *hacked*."

"Nevertheless," Dr. Trent said. He picked up a different folder, this one about the size of a phone book, and sighed as he looked at it. "Would you please ask Mr. Turtell to come in?"

"Sure," I said, still furious about Connor. "Thanks, Dr. Trent," I said, leaving the office. I wasn't sure what I

116

was thanking him for — implying that I might lose my hard-won position as class secretary because I'd been hacked?

I waved goodbye to Turtell, who advised me to "fight the man" and "speak truth to power." I nodded, held up a fist in solidarity, and headed out into the hall, my thoughts racing.

What if it wasn't just a coincidence that Connor had reported my profile to Dr. Trent?

What if he'd been the one who'd hacked it?

He'd been on my list, of course, but I hadn't really believed it was him — I couldn't imagine him doing something so duplicitous, since he was so by-the-rules.

But then again, I reasoned, so was Mussolini.

I texted Ruth the situation, knowing that she'd be in class, but could read it when she got out. Then I pulled out my list and added to it.

Mad's Friendverse Hacker/Possibilities:

1. *Kittson Pearson* — I THINK IT WAS HER!! Motive: wanted Justin, got him, once she got me out of the pic. ☹

2. *Connor Atkins* THINK IT MIGHT HAVE BEEN HIM! Trying to get me kicked off student government, still angry about the recount thing. Bitter that I didn't want to go out with him?

I folded up my list and checked my watch — although I had Latin in twenty minutes, I wanted to get some answers as to how this had happened in the first place. Armed with a Diet Coke, I went to see Frank Dell — hold the Frank.

****

"Can you keep that away from the equipment?" Dell asked, eyeing my can of soda warily. "I can't tell you how many computers I've had to repair because people dump soda on them."

I picked up my DC and held it tightly. Dell worked in the basement, out of what I was pretty sure was a converted maintenance cupboard. At any rate, it was tiny and dark and carried the lingering scent of lemon Pine-Sol. It was also filled with laptops and desktops, keyboards, dismantled hard drives sprouting wires, and pieces of equipment I couldn't even begin to identify, beeping softly and blinking occasionally.

Technically, Dell was doing an elective in computer studies, but everyone knew the reality — Dr. Trent had figured out that it was a lot cheaper to employ a student for credit than have to pay a professional to fix the school's computer glitches. So Dell got two free periods a day to keep PHS wired.

Dell looked like he spent most of his time down in the computer lab, or at least out of the sun. He was shortish and pale and seemed to wear mostly black. I didn't think I'd ever seen him out of a hoodie. His hair was tangled and dread-y, and stood up in many directions, apparently of its own accord.

"So here's the thing," I began.

"Your Friendverse was hacked," he said without looking up from the monitor of the desktop he was rapidly typing on.

"Yes!" I said, relieved I didn't have to give the speech again. "How did you know that?"

"Word gets around, Madison." He paused in his typing and looked at me. "I mean, you misspelled the name of the town we live in."

"*I* didn't," I reminded him. "Someone else did. And you need to tell me how this happened. I mean, how could someone have done this?"

"It's not that difficult," he said, going back to typing. "I assume you have only the standard security measures in place?"

"Um, yes?" While I was better with computers than Ruth was, I could really only do the most basic stuff, and when something went wrong, I tended to give my laptop to someone else to fix rather than trying to figure it out myself.

"That's probably your problem there," he said. "Personally, I have a 128-hex encryption on all my passwords, and I've been doing the same thing for Dr. Trent. It's the only safe way to go."

"Does my computer even have that option?"

"It can," he said, walking over to a laptop and powering it up. "Was your password easy to guess?"

"Not that easy," I said, thinking about how many possibilities that existed for each person's password.

"Well," he said, shrugging, "you can't hack into Friendverse and change people's profiles. They have firewalls even I don't know how to touch."

"Have you tried?" I asked, joking.

"Sure," he said, completely serious. "The only way to get known in this business is to show people the weaknesses in their defenses so you can tell them how to build them up. But Friendverse is solid."

"So someone just guessed?" I asked, surprised and disappointed. I had been hoping that we'd have uncovered some kind of hacking trail that would have led us to the hacker, who we would then bring to justice.

"Most likely," he said. "Unless someone had access to your computer when the hacking happened."

"No," I said, "I was away."

"Then someone probably just guessed," he said. "I mean, they'd have to know the e-mail address you use to log in, and probably something about you. And after you've tried to log in unsuccessfully three times, Friendverse shuts the profile down until you answer an e-mail from them. So they would have had to have a pretty good idea."

"Hmm," I said, pondering this. I'd always figured that the hacker must have known me pretty well — they'd known too much information about my life, and had been able to convince people that they *were* me — but this really drove it home. Who was it?

And more importantly, would I ever find out?

The first bell rang, and Dell began shutting down his various machines. "Well, thanks," I said, heading for the door.

"Certainly," he said. "How's the MacBook holding up?"

"Fine," I said. "Except I still can't type *Q*'s."

"But who needs *Q*?" he asked with a grimace that, for him, seemed to pass for a smile.

"Oh," I said, remembering, "Liz Franklin said her computer was still acting up."

"Oh yeah?" he asked, straightening up. "Did she say anything else?"

"No," I said, "she's kind of pissed at me right now. Why?"

"Nothing," he said, leaning down towards a monitor, his pale face flushing. "Just wondering if she'd had any other problems with it. That's all."

The second bell rang, and I realized that I was now going to be officially *tardus* to Latin. But as I looked at Dell illuminated by the light of the monitor, I remembered what Lisa had speculated yesterday: that Ruth had a crush on him. "Dell," I said, with all the casualness I could muster, "you're not dating anyone, are you?"

"No," he said, looking up at me. Then, leaning back down toward the monitor, so softly that he must have been talking only to himself, I heard him add, "not yet."

CHAPTER 9

Song: Surprise, Surprise/The Starting Line
Quote: "Pineapple is not an appropriate topping for a
pizza." — Big Tony

"Any new prom business?" Kittson asked cheerfully from the front of the classroom where we were having our weekly junior prom committee meeting. It took all my self-control not to fling my after-school snack of SweeTarts (minus the blue ones) at her.

Kittson had decreed, at the start of the meeting, that due to my breaking the "promfidentiality" agreement — which I did not remember agreeing to — by posting insider-committee knowledge on my Friendverse, my status as a member of "the school's most important committee" was now considered probationary. I now could not speak without being spoken to and had to address Kittson as "Chairwoman Pearson." All of which might have been really upsetting if I didn't have so much else to think about.

My head was filled with thoughts of Connor and Dr. Trent and Dell and the fact that Jimmy had — twice — managed to "accidentally" knock my books off my desk in English, and that Liz had turned and started walking the other direction when she saw me heading toward her after classes were over. Also, the fact that Kittson had a huge hickey on her neck, and wasn't even trying to hide it, but was instead wearing one of the lowest-cut shirts I'd ever seen. I was trying not to think about how Justin had probably given the hickey to her, or that most of my *Dane* lines were still unmemorized, or what the real meaning of Nate's haiku could be, and if it could possibly have something to do with me.

"So," Kittson said, banging her pink gavel on the podium and shaking me out of my reverie, "finally, we've come to the moment we've all been waiting for."

I looked at the clock in surprise — I hadn't realized the meeting was over already.

"The final vote on the prom theme!" she continued brightly as she stared daggers at me. She had managed to shoot down all of my prom theme ideas so far, but the votes had always been close. This was because the rest of the committee members were mostly résumé kids who were on the committee just to put it on their applications, and tended to vote with whoever had spoken last.

"Now," she said, her voice growing steely, "I know that . . . some . . . of you have proposed themes that are 'punny.' But I can assure you, there is no place for humor at a prom. This is a special, sacred night that we will treasure always. Therefore, I propose that this year's prom theme should be A Night to Remember."

One of the résumé kids raised his hand. "Wasn't that a Mandy Moore movie?"

"Walk," the girl next to him said, "*A Walk to Remember.*"

"Oh," he said. "Okay then."

"So are we agreed?" Kittson asked. I raised my hand. She glared at me. "Madison?"

"Kittson — I mean, Madame Chairperson —"

"Chairwoman Pearson."

"Right. Sorry. You do realize that's the title of that book about the sinking of the *Titanic*?"

She stared at me. "What?"

"Yeah," I said. "We all had to read it in fifth grade."

"Well," she said, tossing her hair, "nobody remembers that now. *Do you*?" she aggressively asked the rest of the committee, most of whom were engrossed in their PDAs. She seemed to take their silence for consent. "Good. Anyone in dissent?"

I raised my hand, but I was the only one who did. Kittson banged her gavel. "Excellent," she said. "A Night to Remember it is. We're adjourned."

I was a half-second away from asking her if she planned to decorate the ballroom with plastic icebergs and pictures of hypothermic Leonardo DiCaprio when it hit me that she would be going to the prom with Justin.

I had been planning on going to the prom with Justin. And, true, he hadn't asked me, and we hadn't really made any plans, but I had been assuming we would go together. And now he was going to go with Kittson.

Maybe not. Maybe not if I could get to the bottom of this hacking mess. But the thought of them slow-dancing to power ballads was sobering enough to make me lose interest in mocking her theme.

"So now that we've locked down a theme — finally — I can go live with the website. Maybe we can do something with a scrapbooking motif and the captions can be links . . ." Kittson trailed off. The rest of the committee was heading out, no doubt to their next activity.

I remained frozen in my seat and stared at her. "You're doing the website?" I asked. "You know how to do that kind of stuff?"

"Sure," she said with a shrug, packing up her designer messenger bag. "I'm great with computers."

****

"But that doesn't mean anything, Mad," Dave said as he leaned around his stack of pizza boxes to look at me. "Just because she's good with computers doesn't mean she hacked you."

"I know," I said, "but still." We had all convened at Putnam Pizza, where Dave was working, to sit in the restaurant's biggest booth and drink free sodas and watch him fold the flat pieces of cardboard into pizza boxes. Generally, if we hung around long enough, Big Tony, the owner, would bring over a free pie. Which was always excellent, even if he did refuse to serve me pineapple. Tony insisted that fruit had no place on a pizza and hadn't been swayed by my "tomatoes are a fruit, too!" argument. He was also horrified — as were the rest of us — by Ruth's onion-anchovy-ham preference, so he usually just brought over cheese.

Dave had been working at the pizza place for three months now, and we all enjoyed the perks. Dave's father had made him take the job, since he wanted his son to "learn the value of a day's work." What this really meant, though, was that Dave had to deliver pizzas in a BMW that Little Tony was always taking for joyrides without Dave's permission.

"A Night to Remember?" Ruth asked. "That's kind of morbid, isn't it?" she laughed. "What are the favors going to be, Life Savers?"

"My thoughts exactly," I said. I'd known Ruth was going to get it, and not only because we'd done a project on the book together in fifth grade. Because Ruth had been in charge of most of the research, we'd gotten an A. "I'll suggest it at the next meeting."

"Well, I still think Kittson did it," Lisa said firmly. "She wanted Madison's man."

Ruth shook her head. "Please, never say that phrase again."

"But would she have known the rest of that stuff?" Schuyler asked. "I mean, about Jimmy and Liz and my sailing accident and everything?"

"She probably could have found out," Lisa said, and I shifted uncomfortably in my seat. She probably *could* have, due to the fact that people I'd told were apparently not keeping things to themselves.

"So Kittson Pearson was hitting on me?" Dave asked. "Awesome."

Lisa knocked over Dave's stack of boxes. "Whoops. I mean, *houp!*" she said. Dave grumbled and began picking them up.

"But then what was your text about?" Ruth asked. "The one you sent me about Connor?"

"What about Connor?" Schuyler asked, flushing.

"Well, I think he might have done it too," I said as I related what Dr. Trent had told me.

"OMD, Shy, learn your combination," Lisa said when I'd finished the story.

"It certainly sounds like he had a motive," Ruth mused.

"No!" Schuyler said. "Of course he didn't. He was just looking out for the good of the school."

"What is up with you and Connor Atkins?" I asked, looking at Schuyler's beet-red face.

"Nothing. What? Why?" she stammered.

"Well, if you want to shake him down, he's playing a lacrosse game today against Stanwich. He's probably out on the field," Lisa said.

"How do you know that?" Schuyler asked, frowning at Lisa.

"Yeah," said Dave, gripping the cardboard so tightly it seemed in danger of ripping.

"It's a thought," I said, checking my watch.

"Go for it," Ruth said. "Get the dirt. Talk to you later."

"Talk to you soon," I replied, out of habit. "Okay," I said, gathering up my stuff. "I'm off."

"Mads," Schuyler said, looking agitated. "Don't — I mean, when you see him, don't mention —"

At that moment, Big Tony dropped a pizza on the table and whatever Schuyler was saying was lost in the scramble for slices. Since she immediately grabbed one and started eating, it seemed she didn't want to continue the conversation.

I grabbed a slice and then headed out the door without looking back.

I was on a mission, after all.

CHAPTER 10

I headed back to school, eating my pizza as I drove over to the lacrosse fields, which were located behind the main building. I realized as I did so that it'd been a while since I'd been to any kind of sporting event.

Schuyler didn't like us to come to her tennis matches, claiming that our cheering — particularly when it was in French — made her mess up her serve. And after we started going out, I saw no reason to keep going to Justin's rugby matches and pretending I had interest in watching one of the most frightening and violent sports I'd ever experienced. I wondered, with a small pang, if Kittson went to the matches now.

But mostly, it felt nice to be back as I headed over to the field, taking in the people sitting in the bleachers and on blankets, or standing around and drinking the Gatorade and eating the oranges intended for the team.

I took a seat on the bleachers on the Putnam side and checked out the players. I spotted Connor right away; he was in the middle of the field arguing with the ref about something that seemed to be called high-sticking. As I tried not to giggle, I looked closely at Connor. He was actually not bad looking, with dark red hair and a few freckles. He might even have been cute, if only he hadn't been such a jerk.

Proving my point, his yelling got louder, he threw his stick down, and then, it seemed, got yelled at again for unsportsmanlike behavior. As he picked his stick up, he seemed to notice me in the bleachers. I waved at him, but he merely narrowed his eyes at me and went back to playing.

I was suddenly very glad I'd come. Clearly, if the eye-narrowing was anything to go by, he had something against me, which moved him to the top of my suspect list.

I looked around and saw, a few feet down from me, Brian McMahon, holding a notebook and looking fixedly at the field. "Hey Brian," I said, sliding a little bit closer. "What's up?" I knew he was still mad at me — he refused to pass me anything in our Marine Bio labs, much to Marilee's delight, who by now had heard the whole profile story and was watching our unfolding drama with

131

glee. But I was hoping that he was getting closer to forgiving me.

"What's *up*?" he sputtered. "Madison, I'm practically grounded for life because of you. You and your stupid Friendverse comments!"

I sighed. I explained to Brian again that I'd been hacked. "But what did I — the fake I, that is — say to get you grounded?"

"You — or your hacker or whatever — put out all these bulletins about how 'raging' all my parties are and what goes on at them. And posted all these pictures from my bashes. And my dad checks my Friendverse. When he saw all that, he hit the roof. I'm grounded until I'm thirty." As Brian finished saying this, he slumped over, resting his elbows on his knees, clearly overcome by his tale of woe.

"Brian, I'm sorry," I said. "I don't know who did this, or why, but I promise I'm going to find out."

"Well, it must have been someone who's been to my parties, right? Because they knew details and had pictures."

This was not exactly helpful. "But half the school shows up at your parties," I reminded him. "We're not exactly narrowing the field here."

As I said this, something successful and lacrosse-related must have occurred, as everyone on the Putnam side stood and cheered. Brian and I clapped quickly. "Any idea what just happened?" I asked.

"No," he said, frowning. "And I'm supposed to be covering this for the *Pilgrim*." The *Putnam Pilgrim* was the school paper, but I hadn't known Brian was on staff. His extracurriculars had always seemed more confined to stuff like befriending the staff at Karl's Keg Kompany. I mentioned this, and he told me that as part of his grounding, his father was making him participate in more school activities. "I'd better go," he said as the whistle announcing halftime blew.

"One thing," I said, standing up. I needed to ask him what I'd been wondering ever since I saw Nate's profile. "Um, how do you know Nate Ellis?" It was strange for me to say his name out loud — I hadn't done it that often — and I found myself unable to stop smiling as I said it. It must have been because of the "s" sound in "Ellis."

Brian stared at me. "How do *you* know Nate?" he asked. "We went to camp together, a million years ago."

"Oh," I said. "We were on a trip together over spring break, that's all." I saw Brian's eyes light up as I said this.

"So *you're* the girl that —" he said, but then stopped just as it was getting interesting.

"I'm the girl that what?" I asked. "Did Nate say something about me?"

"Ask him yourself," Brian said with a small smile that told me he was glad to be getting even a little bit of revenge for the Friendverse fallout. He pointed across the field to the Stanwich side. "He's right over there."

I looked where Brian was pointing and saw Nate, looking almost unfairly cute, with a camera around his neck, heading across the field toward the Putnam side.

Brian took off toward him, and when he and Nate met halfway, they did a complicated guy handshake and then parted again. As Nate approached the bleachers, it became clear that he was heading in my direction. This made me much more nervous than it really should have.

I mean, I didn't *like* him or anything. He was just a guy with an intriguing profile that I'd eaten ice cream with. But as he got closer, I suddenly thought about how I now knew what his favorite movies were, and that we liked some of the same books, and that I'd never heard of most of his music. And that he'd written a haiku that might — but probably didn't — have something to do with me.

I stood up. I wished I'd reapplied my lip gloss, but knew I couldn't do it now, because it would be really obvious. I hoped I didn't have any pizza in my teeth. As he walked up to me, I could see him smiling, that kind of sarcastic smile that just pulled the corners of his lips up slightly.

I told my heart to stop *thump-thump*ing, but it paid absolutely no attention to me.

"Madison MacDonald, I presume?" Nate asked. As he had been the day before, he was wearing the emo-prep combo that I really liked.

I smiled at him. "Nate the Great," I said, "the boy detective."

"That was Encyclopedia Brown."

"That's right. What are you doing here?"

"I'm the photographer for the *Stanwich Cardinal*," he said. "Our paper."

"How'd you get roped into this assignment?" I asked. Nate didn't really seem like the lacrosse type.

"Slow news day. What are you doing here?" Clearly, I didn't come off like the lacrosse type either.

"Well," I said. I tried to raise one eyebrow at him, Nancy Drew–style, but I think I just contorted my face instead. I'd never been able to get the hang of that one. "I'm about to investigate a suspect."

He looked at me and frowned. "Where's your trench coat?"

"At the cleaners, unfortch."

"Unfortch?"

"Tewtally," I said. "Get with the lingo."

"I think I'll pass." He gave me a wry, surprised smile. "Does this have something to do with your hacking?"

"It does," I said. I pointed out Connor, sitting on the sidelines. "Number twenty-six. I think he may have done it."

"How are you going to find out?"

"I haven't gotten that far yet," I admitted. "Any suggestions?"

He shook his head. "No idea. But for what it's worth, I don't think the techniques they employ on *24* would be advisable."

"I think you're probably —" I stopped when I registered what he'd said, thinking about his Friend-verse profile. "Wait a second. I thought you didn't watch TV."

He stuck his hands in his pockets and looked down at me. I fought back an urge to stand up on the bleachers so I could look down at *him*. "You checked out my profile, huh?"

I could feel my face get hot. "Well, yeah," I said, wishing for a cold breeze to cool my face down. I was suddenly feeling very empathetic with Schuyler.

"I don't watch TV," he said, "but I watch TV shows on DVD."

"But that's the same thing!"

"No it's not."

"Of course it is! You're just being a snob."

He smiled down at me. "Oh, am I?"

I couldn't help smiling back. It was like I was powerless against it, like when you see someone yawn and can't help yawning as well. "You are," I said.

"Well," he said, "maybe someday you and I could . . ."

136

I didn't get to hear the rest of this sentence, because I suddenly noticed, over Nate's nicely broad shoulders, Connor throw his stick down again and storm off the sidelines and toward the parking lot.

"I have to go," I said, grabbing my bag and then biting my lip as I looked at Nate. The wind I had been wishing for a few moments before had finally shown up and was blowing his hair down over his forehead. I had the strongest impulse to reach out and brush it back.

Which was so strange, because I had never wanted to do that with Justin. Probably because I knew my hand would have gotten stuck in the gel. But still. Thankfully, I stopped before following through with the impulse and horribly embarrassing myself.

I tried to remember what Nate had been talking about right before I'd seen Connor. "Um, what were you saying?"

"It's okay," he said, looking — was I just imagining it? — maybe a little disappointed. "Never mind. You have to go interrogate the suspect, huh?"

I nodded. "The game is afoot." I noticed, getting a little panicky, that Connor was almost all the way across the parking lot. "But, um — I mean . . ."

"I'll see you around," he said, and I noticed for the first time how nice his voice was. Kind of low and a little bit gravelly, like he'd just woken up. "I mean, we're friends now. Officially."

"Right," I said, a little shocked at how much I didn't want to leave. But I had to! The suspect was fleeing the premises! "Bye," I said, turning around and hustling toward the parking lot so I wouldn't have to keep looking at Nate and want to stay and listen to his voice and touch his hair or whatever.

"Connor!" I yelled as soon as I got within hearing distance. Even though he was halfway across the parking lot, he stopped putting his lacrosse stuff into the back of a Jeep and narrowed his eyes at me again.

"Madison?" he asked, as though he hadn't just been glaring at me.

"Yes," I said, finally reaching him, a stitch in my side from all that fast walking. "I need to talk to you."

Connor sat down on the edge of the way-back of the Jeep and raised his eyebrows. "What's up?"

I took a minute to notice the unfortunate shininess of his yellow lacrosse shorts. It's really hard to take anyone seriously when they're wearing shiny yellow shorts. "My Friendverse profile."

He stared at me levelly. "What about it?"

I resisted the urge to pick up his lacrosse stick and hit him with it. "It was hacked," I said slowly. "While I was away on spring break. But you know that already, don't you?"

He crossed his arms over his chest. "Maybe."

"You know this because you told Dr. Trent."

Connor continued to stare at me. "So?"

"So," I said, gritting my teeth, "did you do it?"

"Did I do what?"

"Did you hack my profile?" I narrowed my eyes back at him and tried to look for any rapid blinking. "Just tell me. I'm going to find out anyway. I have Frank — I mean, Dell — on the case." Which I technically didn't, but Connor didn't have to know that.

Connor rolled his eyes and laughed. "Of course I didn't hack your profile," he said. "Jesus, Madison. Why would I have wanted to do that?"

I looked at him closely. It certainly didn't seem like he was lying. And I knew he wasn't a very good actor, if his disastrous audition for *The Seagull* had been any indication.

"I don't know," I said, losing a little bit of confidence in my argument. "I thought you were mad about the whole recount thing. And then when I didn't want to go out with you . . ." I said this last part quickly, and could feel myself blushing again.

"Well," Connor said, and I noticed that he was blushing too — you almost couldn't see his freckles anymore. "I mean, I was disappointed in the election results. But I feel I was justified in demanding a recount, as it was a defeat by the slimmest margin in PHS history, according to Dr. Trent."

It took all my willpower not to roll my eyes.

139

"And, yes, I thought you were cute. But when I found out you were going out with that guy —"

"Justin Williamson." I noticed I didn't smile at all when I said Justin's name. but that must just have been because of the lack of *s*'s. At the end, that is.

"Right, him." Connor frowned at me. "And seriously, Madison, that guy? He's such a jock."

"Um," I said, looking down at the shiny yellow shorts.

"I just play lacrosse," he said. "There's a difference between wanting a well-rounded application and being a jock. The point is, when I was told you were dating him, I moved on. I wouldn't have hacked your profile over any of this." He shrugged. "It wasn't that big a deal."

"But . . ." I was trying to process many things.

Like the fact that it seemed like Connor really hadn't done it. That I'd just had one of my two suspects knocked down and was back to square one. The fact that I wasn't such a big deal, apparently. And that when he'd called me cute, he'd used the past tense.

"But you were glaring at me." I knew I was grasping at straws, but I wasn't quite ready to admit defeat yet.

"When?" he asked, looking puzzled.

"Just now."

"Oh," he said, "I can't find my contacts. I can barely see anything. That's why I got kicked out of the game. I was talking about the ref, and didn't see him standing next to me. I need to find them soon, though, or my mom's going to make me get laser surgery, and I really don't want it."

"Oh," I said, starting to feel foolish. Before I could leave, however, I had to get one last question answered. "But why did you tell Dr. Trent about my hacked profile?"

"Oh, that." Connor stood up, finished putting his lacrosse gear into the back of the car and pulled on a black hooded sweatshirt. "I think he felt bad about the whole recount thing. He asked me to be the school's Internet Liaison."

"What's that?" I'd never heard of the position, and was positive that if Lisa had, she would have applied, as she did to anything vaguely French-sounding.

"He just created it," Connor said. "I guess he's been worried about how everyone in school has a Friendverse account. He just wants me to keep an eye out for anything suspicious. And your profile definitely fell into that category."

"Oh," I said, mulling over everything that he'd said. And beginning to feel just how embarassed I was. "Got it. Sorry for the whole false accusation thing."

Connor shrugged and smiled. "It's really okay. I was actually meaning to talk to you. . . ."

I held my breath, hoping he wouldn't try to ask me out. But he wouldn't, right? I mean, he'd used the past tense when calling me cute. "Um, about what?"

Connor blushed again. "Is your friend Schuyler dating anyone right now?"

I let out my breath and told Connor that Schuyler was single, but not in emphatic enough terms to make her sound like a loser. I also told him that he should really avoid any discussion of sailing or boats when talking to her.

Connor thanked me and drove off, leaving me standing in the parking lot. I watched his taillights disappear, then headed to my Jetta.

In the distance, I heard a police siren wail. And then, from the window of an idling SUV that I hadn't previously noticed, I saw a silver Razr arc through the air and smash into fragments on the pavement.

CHAPTER 11

Song: La La Lie/Jack's Mannequin
Quote: "The truth is rarely pure and never simple."
— Oscar Wilde

I walked over to the car. I could see a red-headed girl slouched down in the driver's seat, and I had a feeling that it was Schuyler. Plus, I really couldn't think of another person who would have thrown a phone out a window.

As I got closer, I saw that it was her. Schuyler's eyes were fixed on the rearview mirror, which was angled so it would have shown where I'd just been standing and talking to Connor. I walked over to the passenger door, which luckily had the window down.

"Hey."

She gasped and turned to see me, hand pressed to her chest. "God! Mad!" she said. "You scared me."

"Sorry," I said. I leaned my elbows on the open window base. "I saw the phone, so . . ."

"Yeah." Schuyler shook her head. "It's just total habit now. The car wasn't even moving. I'm like that guy's dog with the bells."

"Pavlov," I supplied.

"Yeah, him." She leaned out the driver's side window, looked down at the shards and sighed. "That was the second one this month."

"Maybe you should just think about one of those hands-free attachments," I said. "It might be a lot cheaper."

"Maybe," she said. She sat up straighter and adjusted the rearview mirror so it was facing the back of the car. "So, um, what's up?"

"You tell me," I said. I watched Schuyler, who was fidgeting and seemed very focused on looking at anything but me. I had been meaning to find out what had been going on with her for a while, and now seemed as good a time as any. "Mind if I get in?"

"Sure."

She unlocked the door, and I climbed into the car, turned in the passenger seat and looked at her. "What's going on, Shy?"

"What do you mean?" she asked, sticking a lock of hair in her mouth.

"Hair," I reminded her.

"Thanks," she said, pulling it up into a messy bun. She fiddled with the stray tendrils. "Nothing's going on. What do you mean?"

"What are you even doing here?"

"I don't know," she said, running her fingers along the steering wheel. "I just, um, wanted some fresh air."

"Shy, come on."

"What?" she sat on her hands. "What makes you think something's going on?"

"Well," I said, "you've been acting kind of weird ever since I got back from spring break. What is it?"

"*Nothing*," she insisted, staring down at the steering wheel.

"Schuyler," I said, "tell me. We tell each other everything." As I watched her continue to stare at her odometer, I felt my stomach drop a little. "Don't we?" Schuyler still refused to look at me, and I flashed through how she had been acting strangely — as though she was hiding something, or guilty about something — since the whole hacking thing began. And a thought so terrible I almost didn't want to say it out loud was crystallizing in my head.

Had Schuyler been the one who'd hacked me?

I had no idea why she would have wanted to, but the rest of it seemed to fit. After all, I'd told her all the secrets the hacker had somehow known.

I sat back against the seat. "Shy," I said slowly. "Did you . . . I mean . . ."

She looked over at me, guilt written all over her face.

"Did you hack me?" I asked, my voice trembling.

"What?" she asked, looking shocked. "Of course not, Madison. How can you even ask that?"

"I don't know —"

"I thought I was one of your best friends —"

"You are!"

"I mean, I know Ruth is your BFF, but I thought I was up there, too. I mean, I was above Lisa in your Top 8 last month. I never would have done that to you!"

I let out a huge breath, incredibly relieved. The thought that I had been betrayed by one of my friends had turned my stomach. "Then what's going on?"

Schuyler sighed. "It's Connor."

That had not been what I'd been expecting to hear. "Connor?"

"Yeah," she said, blushing. "I have a crush on him."

"Connor *Atkins*?"

"Yeah," she said. "He's just so cute, and really sweet and really nice . . ." she trailed off happily.

"Right," I said, trying to give him the benefit of the doubt. Maybe he *was* really sweet and nice when he wasn't accusing you of rigging an election or calling you a kleptocrat.

"But, I mean, I knew he liked you, Mad. So I kind of told him that you were going out with Justin — back when you were, I mean — and that you probably wouldn't be interested." She glanced over at me, guiltily. "I'm really sorry."

"Why?" I asked, genuinely puzzled. "You did me a favor — I *wasn't* interested."

"Oh," Schuyler said. "But I just thought . . . I know that sometimes when one of your friends likes someone, you decide you like them too, and I just didn't want that to happen here."

"No danger of that," I assured her. Then something she had said hit me. "You were speaking about the big-picture 'you,' right? Because I've never done that to a friend."

Schuyler paused for just a second, then said, "Right."

"Shy, I think it's great that you like Connor. I think you guys will be really cute together." I meant it, too. I was just excited Schuyler had decided *she* liked someone, rather than the other way around. And they would look cute together, I realized, with their red hair and freckles. Very Gap ad.

"Really?" she asked, beaming. "Because I like him so much, but don't really know what to do. And I swear I wasn't following you, Mad. I just came over to watch the game and saw you talking." She drummed her fingers on the steering wheel. "So, um, what were you guys talking about?"

I smiled at her. "You."

Schuyler shrieked so loudly, I was glad the windows were down, for the sake of my eardrums. "Really? *Really? I mean, really?*"

"Really," I assured her, and filled her in on the conversation, with Schuyler gasping every third word. "So," I said when I finished, "it seems like you've got a date coming your way soon."

"Omg," she breathed. "This is so exciting! Mad, thank you so much!"

"No problem," I said. I pulled out the list Ruth had made for me from my bag. "Although I'm glad Connor didn't do it, it does mean I'm down to one suspect."

Schuyler peered over at the list. I crossed Connor off and stared down at the only name left: *Kittson Pearson.*

CHAPTER 12

Song: Homewrecker/Gretchen Wilson
Quote: "You want to know what someone's really like?
Check out the cuticles." — Olga the Manicurist

"Fore!" Lisa yelled, lobbing a tennis ball over the court's fence.

"That's golf," Ruth reminded her and she and Schuyler picked up balls from around the perimeter of the court.

Lisa shrugged. "Whatever." Ruth handed her a handful of balls, and Lisa whacked them over the fence.

We were in PE, the only class the four of us had together, on the outdoor tennis courts. Justin had Boys' PE the same period, and I kept looking over to the open gym doors to try and get a glimpse of him.

His class was doing rock climbing on the indoor wall. We had been given a choice this gym class between tennis and rope work, but when Lisa had caught me staring, transfixed, as Justin did pull-ups, she'd hustled us out to the courts.

Truth be told, I wasn't the only one who had been transfixed. Ruth and most of the rest of our class had been staring as well. Justin's triceps were pretty mesmerizing that way. I was just glad that I hadn't been responsible for spotting him. I would have kept spotting the wrong things.

But since we were out on the tennis courts, away from my ex-boyfriend and his delts, this temptation was removed. The four of us were supposed to be playing doubles, but none of us really felt like it, except for Schuyler, and since she was really good, none of the rest of us wanted to play her, so we were simply hitting our balls into the woods behind the tennis courts. This way, when Mrs. Bellus, our gym teacher, came by, we could "go look for them," i.e., continue talking.

"So I checked in with Dell yesterday," I said as I did "froggy in the frying pan," bouncing my ball up and down on a flat racket. Marilee Suarez had been sent to the office after she'd refused to do the exercise on the grounds she was a vegetarian, which had been a highly entertaining beginning to the class.

"Oh yeah?" Ruth asked. "What about? Is your computer still acting up?"

"Yes," I said, "but mostly it was about the hacking thing. But I also," here I threw a sidelong glance at Ruth, "asked him if he was dating anyone."

I saw that Ruth had begun to flush slightly. "What did he say?" she asked.

"He said 'not yet,' which I thought was interesting." I looked closely at my BFF. "Rue, do you like Dell? You can tell us."

Ruth was full-on blushing now, and looked incredibly uncomfortable, all signs that seemed to point to YES.

"*C'est vrai?*" Lisa asked. Her voice rose about an octave. "Really? OMD, this is so exciting!"

"No," Ruth said, fiddling with her initial necklace. "I don't. Seriously. I've just gotten to know him because of our physics project. I don't have a crush on Dell. Okay?"

"Okay," Schuyler said.

"Okay," I said.

"But do you have a crush on *someone*?" Lisa asked. Ruth blushed more deeply. "I knew it!" she yelled. "Who is it? *Qui?*"

Ruth, smiling and shaking her head, opened her mouth to say something.

"Girls!" Mrs. Bellus, sporting one of her multicolored track suits and carrying a clipboard, walked up to the court and stared at the four of us standing clumped in a corner, beyond the baseline. "What are you doing?"

"Tennis?" Schuyler asked, after a pause.

"We lost all our balls," Lisa said, pointing over the fence.

"All of them?" she asked incredulously.

"Yup," Lisa said. "Schuyler here has a mean ace."

Mrs. Bellus rubbed her temples. "Go get them, please," she said as she walked away, shaking her head. The four of us headed out into the wooded area just beyond the court.

"So?" Lisa asked excitedly as soon as we were out of gym teacher earshot.

"No," Ruth said, laughing. "Which is what I was going to tell you. I don't have a crush on anyone right now. But as soon as I do —" she said, maybe in response to Lisa's crestfallen expression, "you guys will be the first to know. Of course."

"*C'est dommage*," Lisa grumbled.

I glanced over at Ruth and tried to raise an eyebrow. She shrugged and mouthed, *Talk to you later.* Which I took to mean that Ruth *did* have a crush on someone, but wanted to talk to me about it first. Which was totally understandable. She was the first one I'd told about my crush on Justin. It was BFF prerogative.

I looked at her closely and wondered who it could be. Ruth was usually pretty private about that stuff, much to the frustration of the rest of us.

"So did I tell you guys about Connor?" Schuyler asked excitedly.

"Yes," Ruth and Lisa chorused, but undeterred, Schuyler launched into the story again.

This time, I added what had happened in terms of my conversation with Connor about the hacking, which Schuyler seemed to feel stole her limelight a little, as she started pouting until Lisa threw a tennis ball at her.

"So if Connor didn't do it —" Lisa started.

"I always knew he didn't do it," said Schuyler a little petulantly, rubbing her head where Lisa had hit her.

"If he didn't do it," Lisa continued, "who did?"

I picked up one of the bright green balls and contemplated the question. "I don't know."

"Kittson," Schuyler said. "Right?"

"Yeah," Ruth said. "She's on the list, right?"

I thought about it. I'd been thinking about it ever since I crossed Connor off. All the pieces fit, everything I'd learned from Agatha Christie et al. — motive, means, intent. Only I wasn't relishing the thought of going up to her in school, probably having to interrupt a makeout session with Justin, and confronting her in public. "Well, I'll talk to her after the next prom meeting, I guess."

Lisa gaped at me. "But that's a week away! You have to act now!"

Schuyler nodded. "Iron while it's hot."

"Girls!" Mrs. Bellus yelled. "Have you found your balls?" This, of course, sent Schuyler into paroxysms (SAT vocab word) of giggles.

Lisa pointed at me. "Madison found one." I held it up as evidence.

"Less talking, please?" Mrs. Bellus said, making a note on her clipboard. I had a sudden fear I had just dropped a letter grade in PE. As soon as she walked away, we began talking again.

"I just don't want to confront her about it in school," I said, grabbing a second ball. "I don't need a big scene with her in the Student Center. People are talking about me enough already."

"Un moment," Lisa said as she took her phone out of her sweatpants pocket and began scrolling though her calendar. "I think Kittson might get her nails done on Wednesdays. I have a standing appointment after my French Appreciation Society meetings, and she's usually leaving as I go in."

Ruth stared at her. "You have a standing appointment?"

"Mais oui," Lisa said. "You would too, if you had my cuticles."

"Mad, you should go!" Schuyler said. "Go talk to her while she can't get up and leave. That's why my step-mother is always buying me spa packages, so she can talk to me while I'm incapacitated in a mud wrap or whatever."

"Interesting idea," I said. I tossed a ball back over the fence, and as I did so, I saw Justin walk to the side of the gym by the doors and begin stretching. He looked flushed and sweaty and really good. Although, I couldn't help but notice, a little bit on the short side.

The bell rang, and we tossed the other two balls we'd found over the fence onto the court. "So?" Schuyler asked. "Are you going to the nail salon?"

Ruth smiled at me. "Go for it," she said.

"It's a plan," Lisa said. "I'll just call Olga and make sure she's free for you after school."

"Okay," I said. "I'll do it." Lisa secured me an appointment, and I resolved to head to Nails "R" We (they had to change the name after they got sued) immediately after school.

After PE, I changed and headed to AP history where I found, to my great surprise and distress, that I had a fifteen-page essay on Queen Victoria due on Friday. But happily, Mr. Karlyle didn't specify font/type size. And whenever that happened, I was a big fan of Courier/14 point, which could turn eight pages into fifteen, no problem.

When the last bell of the day rang, I headed to my locker and saw Liz slamming her door shut and picking up her bag. When she saw me, she paused for a moment, like she was thinking about saying something, but then just turned and walked away.

I had packed my own bag up (trying to ignore the freshgirls two lockers over who were giggling at me) when Sarah Donner walked up to me.

"Hey Mads," she said in a super-sympathetic voice. "How's it *going*?"

I turned and looked down at her. Sarah was about four inches shorter than me, which was one of the reasons she said I shouldn't have gotten the part of Felia, since Josh Burch, who was playing Ham, was about an inch shorter than me. When I'd gotten cast, she'd told Mr. Allan that it would look ridiculous to have the ingénue towering over the leading man. I don't think he cared about the height difference, but I pointed out that as a farm girl in rural Kansas, I'd be barefoot most of the musical, while Ham, who'd just returned from the University of Wittenberg, would no doubt be wearing shoes, which would even out the height difference.

Sarah wasn't bad looking, with long brown hair and blue eyes. She would have been pretty, if only she wasn't so *intense* about everything.

"Hey Sarah," I said. I looked at her outfit, overalls and a bandanna holding back her hair. She dressed normally most of the time, but had been wearing these clothes for rehearsals ever since she read that's all Meryl Streep wore while she was at Yale Drama. "Why are you dressed like that?" I asked. "We don't have rehearsal today."

"I know," she said. "But I'm going to go down to the blackbox to run lines. I'm off-book — of course — but it never hurts to do some extra practicing."

"Right," I said. I really was tempted to tell her not to worry about it, since I would never let her go on for me, but decided against it.

"So how are you holding up?" she asked with a sympathetic head tilt.

"Fine," I said, figuring that she was talking about the hacking. "It all seems to be dying down a little, so that's good."

Sarah furrowed her brow. "Mads, what do you mean 'dying down?' The vote's today, isn't it?"

I stared at her. "What vote?"

"Why, the vote the Thespians are having." She adjusted her bandanna. "A lot of them — myself included, I must admit — were very upset by some of the things you wrote about us on your Friendverse. We're convening to see if someone who's so clearly against the greater good of the Troupe should be permitted to continue as a member."

I couldn't believe this. "Sarah," I said, trying to keep my voice level, "I didn't have anything to do with that. My account was hacked."

She frowned at me, as if in confusion, but I could see she was enjoying every minute of this. "But Mads," she said, "I know you've said things like that before. I'm pretty sure I've even heard you!"

"Yes, but . . ." Why didn't anyone seem to understand that there was a difference between telling one or two people and writing it on the internet? Because it *was* different.

Right?

For the first time, a little seed of doubt about all my information-sharing was planted in my mind.

"I never would have said those things to the Thespians," I said, looking her in the eye. "And I didn't write them on my profile."

"Then you really shouldn't have said it behind their backs, then, should you?" Sarah asked with a little satisfied smile. She looked down at her watch. "Oops, I better get going." She gave me the head tilt again. "Best of luck, Mad. It would be *such* a shame if you had to drop out of the production." With that, she walked off.

I stared down the hallway after her, furious. Sarah was clearly taking her own jealousy out on the other theater kids. But I was also angry at myself for ever saying those things about the Thespians in the first place.

I glanced down at my phone and realized I was going to be late if I didn't hurry to the nail salon. On the way out to my car, I sent a quick e-mail to Mr. Allan explaining what Sarah was doing — because I was almost entirely sure she'd arranged this vote without his permission — and about my hacking and innocent (well, mostly) role in this situation.

Then I sent a text to Ginger, asking her to please vote against Sarah, and to let me know what happened as soon as the meeting was over. I got a smiley face in return, so I could be sure I had at least one vote in my favor.

When I got to Nails "R" We, I saw a pink Mini Cooper in the parking lot with vanity plates that read KIT KAT, so I figured Kittson was inside. I checked my reflection quickly in the rearview mirror, and wished I'd taken the time to put on mascara that morning. When you're going to accuse one of the most popular girls in school of stealing your identity and boyfriend, I had a feeling it helped to look pulled together.

As I walked in, I saw Kittson sitting in the pedicure area, in one of the leather massage chairs, reading *Us Weekly*.

"Hi," I said to the woman at the counter. "I have an appointment with Olga. For a pedicure."

She glanced down at the appointment book in front of her and made a mark on it. "Pick your color, please."

I grabbed the bottle closest to me, a bright crimson. "Here."

She raised her eyebrows at me. "Jungle Red," she said. "Bold choice for this time of year."

As she led me over to the pedicure area, I wondered what she had meant. Was nail polish color *seasonal*?

I didn't have time to reflect on this, however, because suddenly I was sitting in the chair next to Kittson. I still wasn't sure what I was going to say to her. The counter woman told me that Olga would be with me soon, and to put my feet in the water. I rolled up the legs of my jeans and obliged, trying to think of a strategy. I thought back to one of Agatha Christie's most famous detectives and wondered, *WWHPD?* Or, *What Would Hercule Poirot Do?*

"Hello Kittson," I finally said. This was the best I could come up with after trying, and failing, to figure out a strategy.

She looked up from "Stars — They're Just Like US!" and flicked back her long blond hair while her pedicurist massaged her feet. "Oh," she said. "Hey Madison." And with that, she went back to the pictorial evidence of Uma eating a cheeseburger.

If Kittson was guilty, she was certainly hiding it well. I looked at her, trying to discern if she was someone who would be capable of ruining lots of lives just so she could go out with Justin. "I need to talk to you," I said, wishing my friends had come with. I could have used the backup.

Kittson sighed and put down the magazine. "God, Madison," she said, "I'm not changing the prom theme! I've already launched the website."

"No, not that," I said. "Something more personal." I tried to raise one eyebrow and look at her significantly.

160

"Are you okay?" she asked, wrinkling her nose slightly. "Your face is acting weird."

I stopped trying to raise an eyebrow. "I'm fine," I said. "I just wanted to talk to you about something."

"Go for it," she said, picking up the magazine again and flipping through it. "Hey look," she said, angling it toward me, "Reese went shopping."

"Fascinating," I said, trying to stay focused, even though I really wanted to look over and see what she'd bought, "but listen. My Friendverse got hacked over spring break."

"Bummer," Kittson said. She frowned down at the magazine. "Would this shirt work on me?"

"I'm trying to talk to you about something," I said, but glanced over against my will to see the picture of Mary-Kate. "No," I said, "not really."

"I didn't think so," she said, "but it might look cute on my sister." She folded down the corner of the page.

"Listen," I said. "My Friendverse got hacked. Whoever hacked me broke up with Justin. You know," I added significantly, "my *boyfriend*."

"Ex," she said, flipping a page.

"Well, yeah," I conceded, "because whoever hacked me broke up with him. And really messed up my life and a lot of other people's in addition."

"That sucks," she said, looking over at me, "but why are you telling me this?"

161

"I just want to know if you did it," I said, tired of dancing around the situation. The villains in Christie novels were always a lot more forthcoming with their crimes. Also, I was pretty sure none of them had read *Us Weekly* while being interrogated. "If you hacked me."

Kittson rolled her eyes. "Of course I didn't hack you, Madison." She closed the magazine and offered it to me. "I'm done. Want to read it?"

I was torn between my righteous indignation and really wanting to see what Reese had ended up buying. "Thanks," I said, taking the magazine. "But, I mean, just tell me if you did it. I have someone working on the case," I lied, "and I'll find out anyway. And according to Dr. Trent, there will be dire consequences." This was not so much a lie as an assumption. But whatever, Kittson didn't have to know that.

"Madison, no offense, but why would I have wanted to hack you?"

I opened my mouth to reply when my pedicurist came up and introduced herself as Olga.

"Hi Olga," I said, trying to get back to the matter at hand. "Because —" I started to say to Kittson.

"Spa pedicure?" Olga asked.

"Just regular," I said, trying not to spend more money than I had to on a pedicure I hadn't wanted in the first place.

"You should get the spa," Kittson said. "Seriously. It's worth it." She frowned down at my feet. "And it looks like you could use it."

"Regular," I said to Olga. "You would have hacked me because I was going out with —"

"No, really," Kittson said. "They do a whole exfoliation thing and a mask, and —"

"Fine!" I said to Olga. "The spa is fine. Whatever."

"Excellent choice," Olga said. She began sloughing my feet, and I tried not to giggle uncontrollably.

"You won't regret it," Kittson said, picking up *In Touch*.

"Listen," I said, feeling quite sure that Hercule Poirot had also never had to interrogate anyone who apparently had the attention span of a sand flea, while getting a pedicure, "you would have hacked me because you wanted to go out with Justin. And you were mad at me about the whole prom theme thing. And you could have done it — you said at the end of the last committee meeting that you're really good with computers."

Olga looked up at me and raised her eyebrows. Truth be told, it had sounded a lot more convincing in my head.

Kittson smiled as she flipped pages. "Seriously, Madison, if I wanted to go out with Justin I would have just gone out with him. I wouldn't have had to pretend to be someone else on Friendverse to get him to go out with me."

I looked at her — blond, C-cupped, perfect skin — and conceded that she probably had a point.

"Plus, I got the theme I wanted because, no offense, mine was better than yours. And it's a good thing I'm good with computers, because otherwise we would have had to pay what's-his-face to do the website, and you know what the prom budget is like."

"Dell?" I asked.

"Yeah, him. The one who always wears that hoodie. Which, seriously? Ick." She tucked a lock of hair behind her ear. "Anyway, it's not like Justin's this great catch or anything. I've been hooking up with him all year."

I almost kicked Olga in the face as I sat up suddenly. "What? Sorry," I said to Olga, who had begun to swear in Polish. "What?"

"What?" Kittson asked. "It's not like a big thing or anything. Just whenever I was between guys. My friends call him 'Justin Case.' Isn't that funny?"

"Hysterical," I said, my head spinning. Had they been hooking up while we'd been together? I suddenly felt ill, and didn't think it was just from the nail polish fumes. "So were you with him when we — I mean, Justin and I —"

"No," she said, looking more serious that I'd seen her since I'd proposed both *Prom-iscuous* and *Prom-ises, Prom-ises* as themes in a single meeting. "I don't cheat. If he was going out with someone, of course I wasn't going to hook up with him. I didn't even want to hook up with him before he started going out with you, because he was stringing along this one girl. . . ."

"What girl?" I asked. Olga had stopped even pretending to do my feet at this point, and was just listening to the conversation.

"I can't remember," Kittson said. She lowered her magazine and wrinkled her nose. Apparently, this was what she looked like when she was thinking hard. I'd never had the chance to see it before. After a moment, she shrugged. "Nope, can't remember. But seriously? He's not that great. He keeps giving me hickeys. It's *so* seventh grade. I could really use . . . I don't know, more of a bad boy type. I'm thinking about breaking up with him. Do you like this bag?" She angled *In Touch* toward me.

"Yes," I said, distracted, "but it'd be a lot cuter in white."

"Totally!" she folded down the page.

"So you're going to break up with him?" I asked, trying to keep up with everything that had been revealed in this conversation. "You're not going to the prom with him?"

Kittson wrinkled her nose again. "Probably not," she said. "I've already bought my heels, and I think he's too short for them. Ooh, look, Angelina bought groceries."

I sat back in my chair. I believed Kittson. She hadn't hacked me. I hadn't been convinced from the beginning, and since she seemed to have some weird penchant for telling the truth, I believed her now.

But that was suddenly not my biggest concern. Justin had been stringing some girl along? What girl? And he'd been hooking up with Kittson all year?

I knew I hadn't known a ton about Justin when we started going out. But at the time, I'd thought it had been part of his Heathcliff-esque mystery.

Come to think of it, we'd never really talked about all that much. We'd mostly just made out. And I really was with Kittson on the hickey thing.

But Justin and I had a *connection*.

Didn't we?

"You okay?" Kittson asked, looking over. "You look kind of weird."

"Just thinking," I said. Suddenly, I was looking at whole chunks of my relationship with Justin in a different light. What else about him didn't I know? And if Kittson hadn't committed the crime, and Connor hadn't either, who had? "Just trying to figure out who could have hacked me."

"Well," Kittson said, flipping pages again, "first of all, you probably have to figure out who would have cared enough about you — no offense — to do it. Right?"

"Yeah," I agreed. I watched as Olga began to paint my toenails Jungle Red in slow, even strokes. "I'm working on that."

CHAPTER 13

Song: The Quiet Things That No One Ever Knows/
Brand New
Quote: "We do not believe in the possibilities of
defeat. They do not exist." — HRH Queen Victoria

Friendverse Messaging
Nate
4/9 9:30 P.M.   So how's the inquisition going?

Madison
4/9 9:45 P.M.   No luck as of yet. Any advice?

Nate
4/9 9:47 P.M.   "You may think you know what you're
                   dealing with, but believe me, you don't."

Madison
4/9 9:50 P.M.   Thanks. That's really helpful.

Nate
4/9 9:54 P.M.   Quoting! It's from Chinatown.

The movie.

Madison
4/9 9:55 P.M.   You're all about the obscure movies, huh?

Nate
4/9 9:57 P.M.   Always.

Madison
4/9 9:59 P.M.   That's where your screen name comes from, right? The Hitchcock movie?

Nate
4/9 10:01 P.M.   You got it. Except the movie is North by Northwest.

Madison
4/9 10:02 P.M.   I know, I Googled it, and they asked me if that's what I meant to type.

Nate
4/9 10:04 P.M.   You Googled it, huh?

Madison

4/9 10:05 P.M. Um, maybe. So are you planning on being a film major?

Nate

4/9 10:08 P.M. Thinking about it.

Madison

4/9 10:10 P.M. Where are you going next year, anyway?

Nate

4/9 10:12 P.M. Yale.

Madison

4/9 10:13 P.M. Staying close to home, huh?

Nate

4/9 10:15 P.M. I guess so . . . it's also a really great school

Madison

4/9 10:15 P.M. I've heard that ☺

Nate

4/9 10:15 P.M. So what's the plan? In terms of finding the hacker?

Madison

4/9 10:16 P.M. I'm working on it.

Nate

4/9 10:17 P.M. Here's a tip: "Round up the usual suspects."

That's Casablanca.

Madison

4/9 10:19 P.M. Do you only watch movies that begin with "C"?

Nate

4/9 10:21 P.M. You got me. Best of luck with the search.

ttys,

Nate

It was, I found, incredibly difficult to do a report on Queen Victoria when you had just been Friendverse messaging with a very cute guy.

It was even more difficult to concentrate on writing about Queen V because I kept going to my Netflix queue and adding new movies, some of which might have begun with *C*.

And I was finding it especially hard to write my essay on Queen Victoria because my computer refused to type the letter *Q*, which was, unsurprisingly, somewhat crucial to the essay.

After twenty minutes of staring at Nate's messages and trying to decipher hidden meanings in them; trying not to let myself get too excited about the fact that he was going to be only an hour and change away from Putnam at Yale, because what did I care?; deciding that he was mocking me with his final sign-off; wondering what that meant; deciding that it probably didn't mean anything, but if it did mean something, it was maybe good; and attempting to begin my essay by referring to Queen V as "Female Royal Person Victoria," I gave up and turned off my computer.

I checked my phone and saw I had two new texts.

INBOX 1 of 81
From: Ginger Davis
Date: 4/9, 9:17 P.M.
Don't worry! Vote didn't go thru. Mr. A found out & called off meeting. Phewf!!

INBOX 2 of 81
From: Ruth Miller
Date: 4/9, 10:19 P.M.
Hey — I'm going into study mode for physics final Fri.
We'll talk tomorrow, ok? ttyl

I immediately sent a response to Ginger, thanking
her, and then one to Ruth. When Ruth went into her
study mode, she was pretty much in Unabomber mode.
She'd gotten into the habit of alerting me so that I
wouldn't worry or wonder what was up when she didn't
respond to texts or calls.

SENT 1 of 62
To: Ruth Miller
Date: 4/9, 10:25 P.M.
u got it. good luck hitting the books.

ttys!!

I headed downstairs to find my mother and father
both sitting at the kitchen table with their laptops.
My father was wearing the ancient Cubs hat he wore
when he wanted to indicate that he was working on his
column and not to be disturbed. My mother's laptop was
displaying about five different stock reports, all fluctuat-
ing wildly, and she was staring at the screen intently.
"Hey," I said as I grabbed a bottle of water from the
fridge and sat down at the head of the table.

"Hi hon," my mother said without looking up from the screen. My father simply pointed to his hat.

"So I have to write this essay on Queen Victoria that's due on Friday," I said as casually as possible, hoping one or both of them would conveniently forget it was Wednesday.

"Do you need me to proofread it?" my mother asked.

I wished. I supposed I could get her to check that I'd spelled "Female Royal Person Victoria" correctly, but there didn't seem to be much point to that. "Um, I'm not quite that far along yet," I said. "The problem is that my letter *Q* has stopped working. Could I switch laptops with one of you?"

Both my parents looked up at me in alarm.

My father pointed to his hat again. "Madison, I'm in the middle of a column that has to run in tomorrow's paper, which is going to be put to bed very soon. I need to file it in —" he looked up at the microwave clock — "an hour and ten minutes. I don't have time to be switching laptops." And with that, he pulled the brim of his hat down and continued typing furiously.

"You really shouldn't have left this assignment to the last minute," my mother admonished.

I pointed at my father. "Daddy did."

"Yes, well," my mother said, sneaking a glance at her laptop, "this is what comes of having your computer painted without my permission."

I took a sip of water. "So if I'd gotten your permission, this wouldn't have happened?"

"Probably not," my mother said, "because I would have said no."

"Which is exactly why I didn't ask."

She sighed. "Go borrow your brother's computer."

I perked up. This would give me the chance, with full parental authority, to spy on Travis's recent Google searches. "Really?"

"Yes," she said, "but please work upstairs. I think we're bothering your father."

My father was typing with one hand, the other pressed against his ear to block out our conversation.

"Sorry Dad," I said quietly. I took a few York peppermint minis out of the cupboard and headed upstairs. Travis's door was open, but he wasn't inside his freakishly neat room. I walked over to his desk to pick up his laptop when I noticed something crumpled up in the wastebasket under his desk. It was just a piece of notebook paper, but I could have sworn I saw a piece of my name on one of the corners — *adiso*. I figured it was worth investigating.

I had no idea where Travis was — he might have been taking one of his weird hourlong showers that made me glad I had my own bathroom — and I knew he could be coming back at any moment. But I decided to risk it. I sat down on his desk chair and grabbed the paper out of the wastebasket. In my brother's meticulous handwriting was written:

Madisonmacdonald Madison!
Madisonmacdonald macdonaldmac
Madmacdonald justingirl
Theater justingrrl
Justin stupidsister

Oh my God. What the hell was this?

"What are you doing?"

I spun around in the chair and saw Travis standing in the doorway, holding his cell phone. I crumpled the paper in my hand and quickly transferred it to the front pocket of the Putnam Pilgrims Tennis Team sweatshirt I'd stolen — I mean, borrowed — from Schuyler the last time I'd stayed over at her house.

"Nothing," I said, standing. "What's up?"

Travis frowned at me. "What are you doing in my room?"

I tried to look nonchalant. "Oh, Mom said that I could borrow your computer because mine is acting up. But," here I did a big yawn and stretch, "I'm actually kind of tired. I'm going to turn in. But I might have to borrow your computer tomorrow, FYI."

My brother was still frowning, and I noticed that he kept looking down at his cell. "Mom — Mom said that you could use my computer?" he asked.

I was surprised that this was his reaction, as I had been expecting more outrage. But he seemed kind of distracted.

"Yes," I said, looking at him closely and speaking with emphasis. "But I promise I won't do anything to invade your privacy. Because that would *really suck*, wouldn't it?"

Travis looked up from his phone. "What are you talking about?" he asked, looking a little nervous.

"Oh, nothing," I said, staring hard at him for one more moment. "Night," I added, leaving his room and heading down the hall to mine. The piece of paper was burning a hole in my front pocket. I shut my door, climbed up onto my bed, unfolded it, and read it once more.

It was seriously suspicious.

Had the hacker been under my nose the entire time?

Had it been *Travis*?

Pieces were beginning to fall into place: all the time he'd spent on the internet on the ship, the fact that he lived to torment me, his weird comments about whether I'd gotten any interesting e-mails.

Oh, I was going to *kill* my brother. Once I had proof.

I took out my list, crossed Kittson off, and added Travis to it.

Then I looked at his paper — which could only be his attempts to find out my password — and realized that if Travis had managed to figure it out, it must not have been difficult enough.

And considering most of the school now knew I'd been hacked — **ih8hackers!!** probably wasn't obscure enough either.

I gently picked up my laptop and logged on to Friendverse, happy to see that I'd had four new profile views since I'd gone downstairs. I couldn't help wondering if one of them had been from Nate.

I went into my privacy settings to change my password. I needed something nobody would be able to guess, something that nobody knew about. . . .

Taking my cue from Travis's list, I changed my password to **Jonathangirl**, blushing a little as I did so.

Then, trying not to think about my unfinished — technically unstarted — essay, cute Yale-bound guys, or demonic younger brothers, I turned in.

However, once I'd set my alarm and switched off the lights, I realized that I hadn't yet memorized any of my *Dane* lines for the next day's rehearsal.

I spent the next two hours staring at my script and muttering the oddly Midwesternized Shakespeare.

The next day in English, I was trying — and fail-ing — to pay attention to Mr. Underwood talking about *The Mousetrap*, an Agatha Christie play we were supposed to have read. But since I'd been up until two memorizing Felia's song, "Ham, Let Me In," and the mad scene, I hadn't had time to do much more than skim the play.

I had the text open under my notebook, and I hoped it looked like I was really concentrating on my notes, and not trying to catch up on my homework. Not to mention mulling over my brother's possible role as my hacker.

Jimmy was still glaring at me occasionally from under his black PHS hoodie, but he seemed to have lost a little of his anger toward me. His feud with Liz had seem-ingly only intensified, however, at least as far as I could tell from their screen names. Liz's had changed to **Matthew Was Much Much Better Than You'll Ever Be** and Jimmy's had changed to **You're A ************* Slut.** Matthew, on the other hand, had changed his own to **Please Leave Me Out Of This.**

"The longest-running play!" Mr. Underwood yelled, his sudden volume increase making me look up from where I had been trying to figure out whodunit. "Isn't that something? This play is all over the *Guinness Book of World Records.* An understudy worked on this play for fifteen years. Can you imagine that? Fifteen years as an understudy?"

I looked down at the script on my desk, thinking, but not about *The Mousetrap.*

"Fifteen years without your own chance in the spotlight. If there had been a real Christie murder mystery at the theater, I wouldn't have been surprised. I mean, has *All About Eve* taught us nothing? It's always the understudy. They can't be trusted."

I almost gasped out loud at how blind I'd been. It had been right in front of me. Right in front of me, and I hadn't seen it.

The hacker wasn't Travis.

It was Sarah Donner.

It had to be.

She had motive — she was jealous about all the times she had to understudy me, she was especially upset about losing the part of Felia, and she wanted her revenge. She wanted to make me hated by the other theater kids, get me kicked out of Thespians, and make it uncomfortable enough that I would drop out of the production.

She would have known enough, from things I'd said to her and other theater kids, to fake most of the information. I wasn't clear on how she managed to get my password, but maybe she'd just guessed.

I pulled out my increasingly worn list and added to it.

Mad's Friendverse Hacker/Possibilities:
1. ~~Kittson Pearson~~ — I THINK IT WAS HER!! Motive: wanted Justin, got him, once she got me out of the pic. ☹
2. ~~Connor Atkins~~ THINK IT MIGHT HAVE BEEN HIM! Trying to get me kicked off student government, still angry about the recount thing. Bitter I didn't want to go out with him?
3. My stupid ********** little brother!! Could have done it while on ship. Motive: to make my life MISERABLE.
4. Sarah Donner — THINK IT WAS HER! Angry about the whole understudy thing/ jealous I got what she wanted.

As Mr. Underwood had now seemingly forgotten all about *The Mousetrap*, and was ranting about how his ex-wife had loved *All About Eve*, and that should have been his first clue that she was not to be trusted, I stared at the paper more openly.

I had *Dane* rehearsal in — I checked the clock — two hours. And I was certainly going to be having a conversation with Sarah Donner.

After classes mercifully ended for the day, I grabbed a Diet Coke and my SweeTarts (I'd picked out all the blue ones in AP History) and walked through the Student Center, texting my friends as I went, to let them know the sitch.

SENT 1 of 63
To: Schuyler Watson, Lisa Feldman, Ruth Miller
Date: 4/10, 3:05 P.M.
Okay, it's def not Kittson. Am going 2 try & talk 2 Sarah Donner. THINK IT WAS HER. Wish me luck!! ☺

I immediately received texts back from Schuyler and Lisa.

INBOX 1 of 86
From: Schuyler Watson
Date: 4/10, 3:06 P.M.
Really? Not Kittson? Why? What happened? Good luck with Sarah! Want to get coffee later??

INBOX 2 of 87
From: Lisa Feldman
Date: 4/10, 3:07 P.M.
Non — it was TOTALLY Kittson! She's just wily & has convinced u otherwise. Cherchez la femme!

I waited a moment, looking down at my phone, for the text from Ruth. When it didn't come, I figured that she must have had one of her technological mishaps. Or maybe she was still in study mode, or busy.

But that didn't quite feel right to me. There was really no occasion that we wouldn't respond to a text if we hadn't made it clear first that we were going to be occupied. We had texted from dentists' chairs, illegally on airplanes and while driving, during movies, in class, and once, in Lisa's case, during a makeout session with Dave.

So I was sure there was a good reason Ruth wasn't getting back to me. I'd just have to wait until after rehearsal to find out what it was. I had other things to concentrate on — like how to accuse someone I'd once thought of as a friend of willfully trying to wreck my life.

What with all the texting, I was a little late in getting down to rehearsal. The green room was empty, except for Mark Rothmann, who was pacing around the room muttering Larry's lines from the scene where he and Claude plot to kill Ham with an ear of poisoned corn.

Trying not to disturb Mark, I dropped my bag quietly, took out my script and a sweater — the blackbox was always cold — and headed into the lightlock.

Because a blackbox is a theater with no wings or backstage area, the lightlock was a small hallway with doors on both sides designed to keep light from the hallway from spilling out onto the stage. The door to the stage wouldn't open unless the door from the hallway was closed, and there was a switch you could flip that would lock the door from the hallway, in case the door to the stage had been left open.

Since there was (obviously) no light in the lightlock, it was a favored makeout spot among the theater kids, and a lot of the time, you had to try and move as quietly as possible past people kissing in the dark, when all you wanted to do was get onstage. This was particularly challenging in period costume.

The lightlock was deserted. But just after I'd gone through the door from the hallway, it swung open again and Sarah entered, looking surprised to see me.

"Mads," she said. "Hey! I didn't think you were coming to rehearsal today."

Without really thinking about it, I flipped the switch that locked the door from the hallway, and stood blocking the door to the stage. I faced Sarah in the narrow, dark space. I was going to get some answers.

"What are you doing?" Sarah asked. "Don't we — I mean, you — have to be onstage? I think they're doing Ham's "Oh, Felia" song."

"Why did you think I wouldn't be at rehearsal?" I asked. My eyes were adjusting to the lack of light. I could see Sarah, but not clearly, and there were weird spooky shadows all around us.

She shrugged. "I don't know. You were late? Why does it matter?"

"Oh, it matters," I said, my conviction that she had been the hacker growing even stronger. "You have been

184

trying to sabotage me in this part from the beginning," I said. "I guess I just didn't think you'd go this far."

"What?" Sarah scoffed. "The meeting yesterday? Well, thanks to your little e-mail, it got derailed."

"I'm not talking about the meeting," I said. "Although that's part of it. I think you were the one who hacked my Friendverse over spring break, and said all those things about the Thespians."

"Madison, you were the one who said those things about the Thespians."

"Yes, but not on the *internet*!" I yelled. Why was nobody grasping this distinction?

"I didn't hack your profile!" she yelled back. "Why would you think I'd do something like that?"

I was getting really frustrated that people kept asking me this. It was putting my skills as a detective into question. Nobody ever asked Miss Marple that. "Because —" I started.

Sarah shook her head. "God, Madison, give me a little credit. If I have a problem with someone, I tell tell them. I discuss it. I don't have to hack into people's profiles."

A banging on the hallway side of the lightlock made both of us turn. "Hey!" I heard Mark yelling through the door. "Whoever's in there, stop making out and let me in. I have to be onstage!"

Sarah moved to unlock the door, but I stepped in front of the switch. "I don't believe you," I said. "I mean, you clearly have some sort of problem with me, but you're not telling me. You're calling secret meetings to try and get me kicked out of Thespians."

"Hey!" Mark yelled again, this time louder. "Seriously. I have to be onstage, now. Wrap it up in there!"

Sarah crossed her arms. "Fine," she said. "I don't think you deserve this part. I think I'd do a better job. And I'm not going to pretend there wasn't a little bit of *schadenfreude*" (not an SAT word, but one we theater kids all knew from repeated plays of the *Avenue Q* soundtrack) "when you got hacked. But I didn't do it."

As I studied what I could see of Sarah's face in the dim light, it looked like she was telling the truth. I certainly knew what her acting looked like at this point, and this was much more natural, with far fewer hand gestures.

"Really?" I asked.

"Yeah," she said. "But the thing is, I was kind of glad when it happened. Because you do say things about people behind their backs. And a lot of the Thespians were really hurt when they heard what you'd been saying."

My stomach gave another little guilty twist, the kind I'd been feeling a lot of lately. "Yes, but I didn't say it to *them*," I murmured. Truth be told, my argument wasn't sounding so convincing to me anymore.

Sarah shook her head. "It's the same thing. As the Bard tells us, 'Give every man thine ear, but few thy voice; Take each man's censure, but reserve thy judgment.'"

"Right," I said quickly, trying to stop her before she got going. Things were bad enough without her quoting *Hamlet* at me. I sighed. I had been so sure the hacker had been Sarah. Deep down, I was relieved it wasn't, but all I'd really wanted was an answer. "Sorry."

She stuck her hands in her overall pockets. "Me too. I don't think I've been handling losing this part all that well."

"Hey!" Mark was pounding on the door now, his voice breaking. "Seriously, whoever is in there, please let me in! I'm missing my cues!"

Sarah and I looked at each other. "We're okay, right?" I asked.

She hugged me in response. (Theater kids hug a lot.) "We are," she said. "Good luck with finding out who really did it."

"Thanks," I said, reaching around her and flipping the switch. A second later, a wild-eyed Mark barreled in.

As he took in Sarah and me hugging in the lightlock, his kohl-rimmed eyes widened.

"Sorry," he stammered. "I didn't know that . . . that you two . . ."

"No worries, Mark," I said with a small smile at Sarah. He let the hallway door close, and we were able to open the door to the stage. "Also, I like your eyeliner," I added in a whisper.

He smiled at me a little warily. "I can give you tips if you want."

"Maybe!" I said as enthusiastically as I could.

We entered the stage to find Mr. Allan livid, not because we had missed our cues (we hadn't) but because the third scene, with Trudy, Ham, and Claude, had come to a halt. Megin and Jamie, who were playing Trudy and Claude, had apparently broken up the night before and were refusing to stand next to each other, much less kiss the way the script called for them to.

Realizing that I hadn't been missed, I walked to the back row and sat next to Ginger, who was asleep over her sketches. I bundled up in my sweater and opened my script.

Then I pulled out my list and crossed Sarah off.

CHAPTER 14

Song: He Ain't Heavy, He's My Brother/The Hollies
Quote: "Surprises are foolish things." — Jane Austen

My phone rang as I was heading out of rehearsal, saying goodbyes to Ginger, Sarah, Mark and the rest of the theater kids, who seemed to be on the path to forgiving me. Plus, with the whole Megin and Jamie scandal, it was clear I was becoming old news.

I looked down at the display and saw that it was my mother. As I mentally scrolled through anything I might have forgotten to do, or had done that I shouldn't have, I answered the phone.

"Hi Mom," I said, heading over to Judy.

"Hi hon," she said, sounding harried. "Listen, your father's at a night game, and I'm dealing with a potential two-point drop in stabilized inflation and need to be on a conference call for the foreseeable future."

"Oh," I said. "Um, that sucks."

189

"Don't say 'sucks,' Madison," she said, almost by rote. "But I'm going to need you to pick up your brother. And go ahead and grab a pizza or something for dinner. I'm not going to be home until late."

I sighed. I hated picking Travis up, as it allowed junior high school boys the opportunity to make comments — factually accurate comments, no less — about my cup size. "Fine," I said, getting into the car, slamming the door, and turning on the ignition.

"Thanks, sweetie," my mother said. "I owe you one. And listen, don't give Travis too hard a time about that girl he likes. You remember what it was like at that age. . . ."

My ears positively pricked up. "Girl?" I asked, caught somewhere between nausea and the feeling that I'd stumbled onto a gold mine. "What girl?"

If my mother hadn't been so stressed, she absolutely would have noticed the glee creeping into my voice. But she didn't, so I say hooray for a two-point drop in stabilized inflation.

"Oh, he mentioned something to your father last night. Apparently, he wanted advice 'for a friend' about asking someone out. Isn't that sweet?"

"Adorable," I said. "And what was her name, again?"

"Oh," my mother said, sounding more distracted than ever. "I think it was something like Olivia . . .

something. The last name began with a *P,* I think. Pearson, maybe?"

Score. "Good to know," I said, doing a little foot jig.

"Now, Madison," my mother said, clarity coming back into her voice, "I'm telling you this in confidence. Please don't tease your brother about this."

"I wouldn't dream of it," I assured her. "Good luck with the point drop. We'll save you some pizza!"

Then I hung up and began plotting. This was my chance to find out if Travis had been the one who hacked me — and, as an added bonus feature, to get him back for thirteen years of evil Demon Spawn behavior.

Pearson . . . something Kittson had said at the nail salon was ringing a faint bell. I had her number stored in my phone for prom emergencies (she hadn't specified what this meant, and I had been a little afraid to ask). I called it.

She answered after four rings. "Kittson," she said by way of greeting.

"Madison," I replied, thinking maybe this was the new thing.

"Hey. Wait. What?" she asked. "Who is this?"

"Hi Kittson," I said, feeling that her answering system left something to be desired. "It's Madison."

"Hey Madison," she said. "What's up? How are your feet? I was right, right? Wasn't the spa pedicure sooo worth it?"

I glanced down at my bright red toenails. It was odd, to be talking to Kittson like this. Almost like we were . . . not friends, exactly, but something. Somewhere in my brain, I knew I should probably be mad about the whole Justin thing, but I wasn't, really. It was beginning to seem like a long time ago that Justin and I were even together. "Absolutely," I said. "My toes look great. But I had a question —"

"And don't forget," she continued as though I hadn't said anything, "we have a committee meeting on Monday. We need to figure out decorations and glitter colors."

"Right," I said. "I'll be there. But I had a quick question for you. Your sister . . ." I let my voice trail off. I could have sworn Kittson had said something about a sister, but I wasn't 100% sure.

"Olivia?" she said. "God. What did she do this time?"

"Oh, nothing," I said, feeling a grin spreading over my face. "I was just wondering if you'd bought her that top. I thought it was cute, but didn't want to get it if she had it too." This made no rational sense at all, but I had a feeling it would be logical to Kittson.

"No," she said, "she so doesn't deserve presents right now. She's being a brat. I think she has a crush on some guy."

"Interesting," I said. I was a heartbeat away from asking Kittson what she had decided to do about Justin —

if they were still going out, if they were going to the prom together — but I restrained myself. "Well, I gotta go," I said, glancing at the Jetta's clock. Rehearsal had run a little long, and I was late to pick up TDS.

"Me too," she said "The *Hills*-athon is about to start. Don't forget about the meeting. Later!" With that, she hung up.

I did a quick Google search on my phone and found the address I was looking for. Then I pulled a piece of paper out of my bag and stuck it in the cup holder. Finally, I revved the engine and headed to Putnam Middle School, which was only a few blocks away from the high school.

Thankfully, because I was late, none of Travis's pre-adolescent cronies were around to make fun of me. There was just Travis, sitting sullenly on the bench by the entrance. When I pulled up he walked over to the car and got in, slamming the door much harder than necessary.

"Where's Mom?" he asked, slouching down in the passenger seat and changing the song on the iCar.

"She had to work," I said. I glanced down at the address on my screen and began to drive in the direction of 65 Lakeview Drive. "But she said we should pick up pizza for dinner. Sound okay?"

"Whatever," he said, pulling out his PSP and beginning to blow things up.

"So Travis," I said casually as we headed in the opposite direction of Putnam Pizza, "you sure were online a lot while we were in the Galápagos."

"I guess," he muttered, continuing to wage war against the tiny aliens.

"What were you doing online, all that time?"

"What do you care?" he asked, turning up the volume on the iCar.

I turned it down. "Just curious," I said. "I also didn't know if you wanted to explain this," I said, pulling the paper I'd found in his room last night out of the cupholder and tossing it at him.

His eyes widened when he saw it. "Where did you get this?"

"From your trash can," I said. "Care to explain?"

"You stole this out of my room!"

"It's you trying to figure my password out, isn't it?" Travis was silent, which I took as a confirmation. "My Friendverse got hacked while we were on spring break," I said. "Someone who really wanted to hurt me did it."

Travis was still staring straight ahead. The ignored aliens on his PSP were probably gaining in force and numbers to take over the planet.

"Did you do it?" I asked, taking a turn a little more sharply than I technically needed to. "You'd better tell me."

194

Travis smirked at me. "Or what?" he asked. "You'll tell Mom and Dad? Ooh, I'm so scared. I'll just tell them you *stole* that paper out of my room."

"No, not Mom and Dad," I said conversationally, making the turn onto Lakeview Drive. "But we're heading toward Olivia Pearson's house right now. You know, the girl you have a crush on?" I was rewarded by seeing Travis's face turn bright red, then super pale, in the course of about four seconds.

"How did you know that?" Travis asked, his voice cracking.

"Oh, I have my ways," I said. "But unless you want me to tell her all about how much you like her, you'd better tell me the truth."

"You wouldn't," Travis croaked, growing even paler.

"You want to try me?" I asked. I pointed ahead to the mailbox bearing the number 65. "We're almost there. I'm sure she'd love to hear all about how you were asking your *dad* for advice on how to ask her out. . . ."

"No!" Travis cried. "I'll talk, okay? I promise. Let's just go, now, before she sees me."

"Promise?" I asked. I swerved close to the driveway and tapped my finger lightly on the horn.

"I promise, I promise!" Travis babbled. "I swear! Just please, go, Madison!"

I paused for one moment, as if considering it, just to get him back for all the things he'd done to me over the years. Then I removed my hand from the horn and made a U-turn. "Fine," I said. "Start talking."

"I didn't hack you," Travis said quietly, still about five shades paler than he normally was, but gaining some color back the further we got from 65 Lakeview Drive. "I promise. I didn't even know you'd been hacked until you told me right now."

"So what's with the paper?"

"Just because I didn't hack you doesn't mean I haven't tried," he said with a smirk. "But I never got it right."

I made the left that would take us back to the center of town, and Putnam Pizza. "So what were you doing online the whole time we were on the ship?"

"Oh," he said, now beginning to blush a little. Travis's complexion was getting quite the workout today. "I was trying to send an e-mail to Olivia."

I noticed that Travis said her name in the tones he usually reserved for words like "Tony Hawk" and "Doritos."

"The whole time?" I asked skeptically.

"Yeah," he muttered. "Everything I tried to write ended up sounding stupid, so I never sent anything. Well," he amended, "I sent your e-mail address to some spam websites, but that's it. Have you been getting any offers to refinance your home or get a super cheap loan?"

"No," I said, glaring at him, "but I guess I have that to look forward to now. Don't do that stuff anymore. I still have her sister's phone number," I added when it looked like he was going to say something snarky.

Travis nodded. "Fine," he said grudgingly.

We pulled into the parking lot of Putnam Pizza, went inside, and placed our order. Dave wasn't there, but neither was Big Tony, so it looked like I had a fighting shot at getting pineapple on my half.

We went outside to wait on the patio. As Putnam Pizza was next to Gofer Ice Cream, my eyes kept drifting over to where Nate and I had sat and had ice cream. Was it only three days ago? It felt like I'd known him much longer than that, somehow.

"So you won't tell?" Travis asked after a moment of silence. "Olivia? Or her sister?"

I crossed my heart. "I promise, as long as *you* promise to stop trying to hack me. Deal?"

He nodded. "Deal."

"So why do you like this girl?"

Travis rolled his eyes at me. "Um, because she's the hottest girl in eighth grade."

"Is that it?" I asked. "Really?"

Travis began to blush again. I tried not to enjoy the spectacle too much. "No," he said. "I mean, she's totally hot. I mean, really hot. But she's really nice, too. And she always laughs at my jokes. I don't know," he said, shoving his hands into his pockets. "I just do, okay?"

"Sure," I said. "And just so you know, when I spoke to her sister earlier, she said she thought that Olivia had a crush on some guy."

"Yeah?" Travis asked, looking really interested, but trying not to look at all interested.

"Yeah," I said, "and maybe you're that guy!" We sat in silence for a second, and then I said, "I could ask for you, if you want. Subtly." I wasn't sure that Kittson would actually understand the concept of subtle, but I could give it a shot.

Travis nodded so vigorously, he resembled Ruth's bobble-headed Darwin. "Yeah," he said, "that might be cool."

"Right," I said. "But listen. Don't go out with someone just because they're hot. You want to go out with someone that you can talk to, someone who shares your interests, someone who makes you laugh —"

"Pizza's up!" Little Tony yelled through the open door, and Travis jumped up to get the pie.

I found my gaze wandering over to the bench where Nate and I had sat. I suddenly realized that when I'd been describing the right kind of person to like, I hadn't been talking about Justin at all.

I'd been talking about Nate.

CHAPTER 15

Song: The Wind Beneath My Wings/Bette Midler
Quote: "Friends may come and go, but enemies accumulate." — Thomas Jones

It was hard to write a history paper on Queen Victoria, I found, when your friends wanted you to IM with them and refused to take no for an answer.

La Lisse:	Mad, you're there?
madmac:	Here. But I have a HUGE paper due tomorrow that I haven't started. So I can't be on too long.
ruthless:	Sorry I missed the text earlier! I was meeting w my study group. How'd it go with Sarah?
madmac:	Exonerated.
La Lisse:	Vraiment?
madmac:	Really. And Travis didn't do it either.
misswatson:	So what now?
madmac:	No idea. ☹
ruthless:	We'll figure it out.

La Lisse:	Mad, what's going on with ice cream boy?
misswatson:	Who?
madmac:	Nate?
La Lisse:	Of course Nate.
madmac:	We haven't talked. But we messaged a little last night. He's going to Yale next year!
misswatson:	That means he's smart!
La Lisse:	Well, we knew that already.
ruthless:	We only know what Mad's told us.
ruthless:	Who knows, she might have been lying to make him seem like more of a catch. ☺
madmac:	Hey!
ruthless:	j/k
madmac:	No, he's really smart and cute. I don't know . . .
La Lisse:	I think someone's a SK!
misswatson:	????? Translate?
La Lisse:	Smitten kitten!
misswatson:	Ooh, who?
La Lisse:	Madison
misswatson:	Oh. But what about Justin?
ruthless:	Shy makes a good point . . . what ABOUT Justin?
madmac:	Nothing! I just think Nate's interesting, that's all.
La Lisse:	"Interesting," hmm? ♥♥♥
madmac:	Oh, stop it.
misswatson:	Omg that's so cute! Lisa, how did you do that?

ruthless:	Well, we're going to have to check out his profile so that we can see for ourselves.
misswatson:	Great idea!
misswatson:	How do we do that?
madmac:	His profile's set to private.
La Lisse:	Mad, just tell us your password and we'll log in as you and check it out.
madmac:	Um, no offense guys, but I'd be worried that someone would hack this chat and tomorrow there'd be bulletins telling everyone I'm dropping out of school to be a pole dancer.
La Lisse:	Good point.
misswatson:	You're not, though, right, Mad? The whole pole dancing thing??
madmac:	NO! This is how rumors get started!
La Lisse:	Why don't we just go to the computer center and you can log in and we can check out his prof?
ruthless:	They've blocked Friendverse from all the school computers.
madmac:	Really?
misswatson:	Bummer!
La Lisse:	And how do you know that, Rue? ♥ Hmm?? Might it have something to do with . . . DELL? ♥♥♥♥♥
misswatson:	୶!
madmac:	???
misswatson:	Oh, shoot, I was trying to do a heart, too . . . hold on . . .

ruthless: Mad, just bring your laptop into school
                tomorrow, and then you can log on to the
                wireless and we can see the prof.
madmac: My computer's pretty fragile
                right now. . . .
La Lisse: Oh, come on!
misswatson: 🔔! 📖! 🧴!!!
madmac: I guess I could. . . .
La Lisse: Tres bien!
ruthless: Great! Gotta go, I have to study for
                physics.
madmac: Me too. History paper, blech.
misswatson: ✈! ☎!! ☄??
misswatson: ☹.
La Lisse: Shy, I don't even know where you're find-
                ing these.
misswatson: I give up.
ruthless: Okay, Mad, so we'll meet you before
                school at your locker?
madmac: Plan!
La Lisse: D'accord.
ruthless: Wish me luck!
madmac: LUCK!
ruthless logged off 9:45 P.M.
La Lisse: Au revoir!
La Lisse logged off 9:46 P.M.
madmac: Okay, Shy, I gotta go write a paper.
misswatson: ♥
madmac: Congrats!
misswatson: I did it!! ♥♥♥ !!!!
madmac: Speaking of which, anything going on
                between you and Connor?

misswatson:	Not much. Just that we have a date tomorrow night!!! !! ♥♥♥♥♥♥♥♥♥♥♥♥♥♥♥♥♥♥♥!!!!!!!!!!!!!!!!!!!!!
madmac:	I want details tomorrow!
misswatson:	Absolute! Night, Mad! Good luck with your paper.
madmac:	Night, Shy.

misswatson logged off 9:48 P.M.
madmac logged off 9:49 P.M.

****

"Hey," I whispered into the phone as soon as Ruth answered her cell. I glanced at the clock; it was 3:30 A.M.

I'd technically gone to bed half an hour before, having written an incredibly bad paper I planned to get up early and fix. But even though it was super late, I'd just been lying awake, staring at the glow-in-the-dark stars Ruth and I had applied to my ceiling when we were in seventh grade. Unable to sleep, I'd logged on to Friendverse and seen that Ruth had just updated her status to **RueRue is ready for her physics test!** so I had hoped she'd still be awake. "Did I wake you up?"

She laughed. "Of course not." Ruth was a semi-insomniac; she'd go through long phases of barely sleeping at all. It was due to this that she knew more than just

203

about anyone else. Whenever she couldn't sleep, she'd stay up for hours, watching the Discovery and History channels.

"Can't sleep?"

"It's been pretty bad lately."

"Well, what are they doing on the History Channel these days?"

"The Spanish-American War. Not that exciting," she said, and I could hear the sound of her flipping channels. The fact that Ruth had a TV in her bedroom was one of the things I was most jealous of. My parents refused to let me have one, and watching DVDs on my laptop just wasn't the same thing. "Why are you up? The paper?"

"No," I said. "That's done. Well, *done* might be too strong a word." I sat up and pulled my quilt over my knees. "Just thinking, I guess."

Her voice was sympathetic. "About the hacking thing?"

I sighed. "Yeah. I'm acting like an idiot, accusing all these people who had nothing to do with it. I just want to know who it was."

"I know," she said. "But if it's any consolation, I think people at school really are beginning to forget about it."

"Jimmy and Liz haven't."

"Well, aside from them."

"But *I'm* not going to forget about it! And I'm seriously out of suspects, so I don't know what to do at this point."

"Move on?" she asked. I could hear a smile in her voice as she added, "Get Dell to install some extra security on your computer?"

"Right," I said. "I'll try."

"Good."

"So are you going to talk about it?" I asked.

"About what?"

"About your mystery crush! The one you mentioned in PE . . ."

"Oh, that." Ruth sighed. "There's really nobody. I was mostly just tormenting Lisa."

"Really?" I was disappointed. "I thought that you were telling the truth."

"Well," Ruth said after a moment. "There's . . . someone . . . I've been thinking about for a while. But I'm not ready to talk about it yet. But as soon as I am, I'll tell you, okay?"

"Well, of course," I said. "We tell each other everything." The sound of the channel flipping stopped, and I could hear dialogue that sounded familiar. "What are you watching?"

"*Beaches*," Ruth said, sounding sheepish.

"*Beaches*!" I cried. "Oh my God, I haven't seen it in years. What part?" Ruth and I had gone through a big

Beaches phase in sixth grade, when we had watched it whenever we'd had a sleepover (which was pretty much every Friday night). I used to be able to quote most of it by heart.

"They're fighting about the fact that Barbara Hershey slept with the cute director."

"Who wasn't even that cute."

"In your, mistaken, opinion."

"And it was completely wrong to fight about," I said, pulling my quilt up to my shoulders, picturing the movie in my head. "Because, I mean, Bette Midler never told Barbara Hershey that she liked him. They weren't dating. It wasn't like he was off limits or anything."

"But a real friend would have known, don't you think?" Ruth asked. I heard the remote click again, and the volume on the TV got louder.

"I don't know," I said with a yawn. "I guess."

"You sound tired."

"Yeah. Getting there."

"Well, it is almost four."

"I know."

"They're at the bra song," she said. "Want to hear it?"

"Please," I said. I'd always loved the bra song. Ruth turned up the volume and held the phone closer to the TV, and we listened to Bette belting it out. "Thanks," I said, when it was over. I yawned again, the fact that it was almost four A.M. beginning to hit me. "I'm going to turn in."

"Good idea," she said. "Talk to you later."

"Talk to you soon," I replied, and hung up. And after that, I got to sleep. For a whole two hours.

****

When I arrived at my locker the next morning, my friends were all there waiting for me. I was chugging a Stubbs latte for all it was worth, to try and make up for my sleep deprivation. When I'd looked at my essay in the cold light of morning, it was slightly worrisome. I'd done it in 14-point Courier, with two-and-a-half-inch margins, finally concluding that Queen Victoria (I'd used my father's laptop so that I could type that essential phrase) had run into problems with the populace because her ideas were too Victorian.

"Well?" Schuyler asked excitedly. "Did you bring your laptop?"

I tapped my big Pilgrim Bank canvas bag. "It's in here."

Lisa rolled her eyes. "Calm down, Shy," she said. "It's just a laptop. Mad, hurry up."

Ruth just shook her head at all of us and continued to peruse her AP Physics notes.

"I'd rather hear about Shy's date," I said.

Schuyler shook her head and pointed at my bag. "Laptop!"

I was happy that they were all so interested in Nate, but a little bit nervous about showing them his profile. What if they only thought he was *kind*-of cute, as I once foolishly had? Then I wondered why I suddenly cared so much. I mean, he was just a friend.

"Let's see!" Schuyler said, reaching for my bag. I pulled out the pink laptop and was just about to open it when the first bell rang.

"*Bof*!" Lisa cried. "*C'est dommage, non? Mais c'est la vie.*" She gave a one-armed shrug. "*Maintenant, je vais à la classe d'anglais. À tout à l'heure!*" With that, she gave a wave and headed down the hall.

I stared after her. "You know, I think she's getting worse."

Schuyler looked crestfallen. "Mad, I wanted to see his profile! I was totally looking forward to it!"

"At lunch," I promised her. "And when are we going to talk about Connor?"

Ruth was still flipping through her physics notes. "Maddie, do you have any opens before lunch? We could check it out then."

I thought about telling Ruth not to call me Maddie, but I decided I just didn't have the energy. Not all of us, after all, had her insomniac's stamina. "No opens this morning," I said, yawning. "Which is too bad, because I really could have used a nap."

If you had an open, and went to the school nurse and told her you were having "female problems," she totally let you sleep on one of the curtained cots for an hour. And she didn't even keep track, so you could go multiple times over the course of the month without her catching on. This made me a little more nervous about her ability to actually, you know, diagnose something, but in the meantime it was super helpful.

The bell rang, and Schuyler and Ruth headed to their classes. I looked sorrowfully at my incomprehensible essay, noticing as I did so three spelling mistakes that spell-check hadn't caught, because they were actual words, just used in the wrong context.

I sighed and locked my laptop in my locker. As I was giving the lock one last spin, Liz rushed up and began twirling her combination. She seemed to be in a hurry — as I probably should have been, too, but I wasn't yet awake enough to move quickly — so I didn't want to bother her with more pleas for a restored friendship.

But when she looked over at me, I gave her a small smile, and after a moment, she gave me a tiny one back, so I hoped that maybe we were on our way to becoming friends again. When the final, Seriously-Why-Aren't-You-In-Class-Yet?! bell rang, I chugged the rest of my coffee and headed to Marine Biology.

Luckily, Brian didn't seem to mind that I kept staring into space, falling half-asleep when I was supposed to be figuring out the chemical properties of seawater. And Marilee was texting madly under the lab table about some drama I was sure I'd hear about in a few days, after she verified her sources.

When I heard Brian say the word "party," however, I woke up a little. "What?" I asked, snapping my head up and quickly checking the corners of my mouth to make sure I hadn't drooled. "What did you say, Brian?"

Brian frowned down at my tilting beaker. "Careful with that," he said. He glanced over at Marilee, whose thumbs were still flying over her keypad, and lowered his voice. "I was just telling you that I'm having a small — *small* — get-together tomorrow night."

"Really?" I placed the beaker in the beaker tube holder. "I thought you were grounded until the next millennium."

"I was," he said. "Technically, I still am. But my parents are at Canyon Ranch's Slim Down and Shape Up Weekend, and I have the place to myself."

I was beginning to think that Brian was not the fastest learner. Although I probably should have guessed this from the first three C- lab reports I let him write. "Um, Brian," I said just as Dr. Daniels walked by. I picked up the beaker and started stirring vigorously, holding it up to the light, the way I'd seen scientists (well, actors playing scientists) do on commercials. Brian and Marilee leaned forward intently, both frowning slightly. I guess we must have convinced Dr. Daniels, because she continued on to investigate the burning smell that had suddenly started emanating from the other side of the classroom. As soon as she was out of earshot, I put the beaker down again and Marilee went back to her texting.

"Is this really the best time to have a party, when you got into so much trouble for your last one?"

"No thanks to you," Brian pointed out.

"Fake me," I countered. "I'd love to go to your shindig, I just don't want you to get into any more trouble."

"Thanks," he said, "but I've got it under control. I've told our housekeeper that I'm having a study group over, so she's going to take the night off. And it's really just a small party — so don't invite anyone, okay?"

"But Ruth can come, right?"

"Doesn't she always tag along with you?"

"Awesome," I said. "We'll be there." It was on the tip of my tongue to ask if Justin would be there too. It was a pretty safe bet — he usually showed up at Brian's parties. But I didn't ask, because suddenly I wasn't sure that I wanted him to be there.

A second later, my brain started functioning again. Of *course* I wanted Justin there. But whenever I tried to picture his face, I couldn't seem to get a clear picture of it. He kept becoming taller and darker-haired somehow.

I sent a quick text to Ruth to let her know about the party, and went to history to turn in the World's Worst Paper.

The rest of the morning passed uneventfully, except for a surprising request for an essay rewrite from Ms. Patterson, my Latin teacher. Apparently, she had not appreciated the theory that the Trojan Horse had been civilization's first prank, paving the way for such luminaries as Johnny Knoxville, the College Humor guys, and Ashton Kutcher. She also hadn't seemed to like my theory that Q.E.D. was actually just the first TLA.

When we'd gone over the declarative tense and she'd berated us for our "frivolous" essay topics, we were allowed to leave fifteen minutes early. I took full advantage of the fact that the food court had just opened, and the good chips were still available. After I'd gotten lunch, I headed to my locker to retrieve my laptop.

I spun my combination and opened my locker to find the usual messy array of papers and gym clothes.

But my laptop wasn't there.

CHAPTER 16

Song: Great Lengths/The Lucksmiths
Quote: "All human situations have their inconveniences."
— Benjamin Franklin

I stared into my locker, frozen, for a few seconds.

I really didn't understand what was happening. I checked to make sure it was, in fact, my locker. It was.

And also, how would I have been able to open it if it wasn't?

Oh, my mother was going to *kill* me.

But how had my laptop been stolen? My locker had been locked — I remembered locking it. The lock didn't look tampered with.

"Oh my God," I murmured, my heart pounding. I shut my locker door and leaned back against it.

"Mad?" Schuyler bounded up, looking excited. My face must have betrayed some of what I'd been feeling, however, because she immediately stopped looking excited and started looking worried. "What's wrong?"

"My laptop," I said, feeling like I was about to cry, "isn't in my locker. I think someone stole it."

Schuyler blinked at me. "Are you sure?" she asked. "I mean, did you check under all your gym clothes or whatever?"

I spun my combination and opened the locker again, lifting up my gym clothes and piles of paper. The laptop had not miraculously appeared.

"You should go to the office," Schuyler said after we'd stared into my locker for a few moments. "They'll know what to do."

I shook my head. "I doubt that highly." I was trying to hold back my panic. My laptop had been stolen. What was I going to do? Even if it didn't type the letter *Q*, it was still my laptop, and who would have wanted to take it? I mean, it was *pink*.

"Go to the office," Schuyler said. "Who knows, maybe there are hidden cameras by your locker and everything was caught on video! Like in Vegas!"

"Okay," I said. I couldn't think of what else to do. "I'll go."

"I'll tell Lisa and Ruth, and then we'll meet you there, okay?" Schuyler said.

"Okay," I said again, feeling a little dazed. Then I remembered that the bell still hadn't rung, and yet there was Schuyler. "Why aren't you in class?" I asked.

"I had an open," she said. She pointed down the hallway. "Go to the office! They say the first few hours after a crime are the most crucial!"

Following Schuyler's advice, but feeling strongly that she'd been watching too much *CSI*, I walked down to the office, only to find the desk vacant and the office deserted except for Glen Turtell.

"Sup, Mad?" Turtell asked, as the bell rang.

"Sup, Glen," I said, sitting next to him on his bench, and careful not to sit on his name, or on the small portrait of himself that had been rendered since the last time I'd been there. As I admired the portrait, I caught a glimpse of his black backpack between his feet. It was open and, I could see, filled with Metallica CDs.

"How'd you get your CDs back?" I asked. "I thought you said Shauna stole them."

Before he could answer, Stephanie came in, carrying a sandwich. She sighed when she saw Turtell and raised her eyebrows at me. "Miss MacDonald," she said, "twice in one week. To what do we owe the pleasure?"

"My laptop was stolen out of my locker," I said. Out of my peripheral vision, I saw Turtell look up suddenly.

"Are you sure?" Stephanie asked.

"Yes," I said, wondering how anyone could be mistaken about something like that.

She glanced toward the door of Dr. Trent's office. "Dr. Trent is with . . . a student right now, but let me tell him what's happening. This is the third theft this week." She disappeared into Dr. Trent's office, leaving me sitting next to a suddenly agitated Turtell.

"Glen?" I asked, as I looked over at him, cracking his knuckles again and again. "Everything okay?"

"No," he said. "Mad, this locker thing —"

Before he could finish, Schuyler and Lisa walked in, talking loudly.

"Did you find out who did it? Did they have it on video?" Schuyler asked me. She saw Turtell and her eyes widened. "Omg, was it Glen?" she whispered loudly.

"You know, I can hear you," Turtell said.

"*J'accuse!*" Lisa said, pointing a manicured nail at him. "Why did you do it?"

"I didn't steal Madison's laptop," Turtell said in a serious, measured voice that seemed to shut Lisa up. "Or any of the other stuff!" he said this loudly, and toward the direction of Dr. Trent's office.

"I just can't believe this," Lisa said, sitting next to me. "I mean, is there no safety in our own school? We need to call in the *gendarmes*!"

Turtell stared at her. "The who?"

At that moment, Dr. Trent and Stephanie came out of his office, with Dell following behind them.

216

"I have to attend to something," Dr. Trent said to Dell. "We'll finish this later."

"Certainly," Dell said. As he left, he nodded at me and exchanged a loaded look with Turtell that I couldn't quite read.

Dr. Trent, looking grimmer than usual, turned his attention to me. "Madison, you're reporting a theft?" he asked.

"Yes," I said, and told him the details of my discovery of my empty locker.

"But how would someone have gotten in?" he asked. "Did any of your friends have your combination?" His eyes slid over to Schuyler, who hid behind Lisa.

"No," I said. "None of them have my combination." Suddenly, I remembered Liz. She knew my combination, but she couldn't have done this, could she? Was she *that* mad about the hacking? I decided not to tell Dr. Trent, and just try and talk to Liz myself later. If it wasn't her, there was no reason to get her in trouble.

Looking around at my friends, I suddenly realized that Ruth hadn't come down with Schuyler and Lisa. But I had bigger things to think about at the moment.

"Was your lock broken?" Dr. Trent asked.

"No," I said. "It looks like it was just opened normally."

"But how could somebody have gotten your combination?" he asked.

"Exactly!" Lisa said.

Dr. Trent frowned at her. "All the combinations are stored in a secure database," he said in a very clipped voice. "There's no way that anybody could have accessed them."

I saw, out of the corner of my eye, Turtell look up suddenly, then begin cracking his knuckles again.

"Don't you have a video surveillance system?" Schuyler asked hopefully. "You know, like they do in Vegas?" She looked around eagerly, as if expecting to see the door to the crow's nest behind Stephanie's desk.

"No," Dr. Trent said shortly. "We don't. Madison, if you could please take me to your locker?"

"Sure," I said. I led the way, with Dr. Trent, Stephanie, Lisa, Schuyler (still muttering about how tighter security saved laptops), and Turtell, who apparently had decided to come, following behind.

I spun my combination, opened the door — and saw my laptop sitting inside, exactly where I'd left it.

I gasped.

Dr. Trent glared at me. "Is this some kind of prank, young lady?" he asked. Stephanie then told him that, according to the new school-board-approved, gender-neutral language codes of conduct, the phrase "young lady" was no longer acceptable. Dr. Trent then said some other things that I also don't think would have been on the school board's list of approved language.

"No, no," I said, staring into my locker, my laptop sitting there, looking pink and innocent, as though it had never been gone. "It wasn't here, I swear."

"It wasn't!" Schuyler, bless her, piped up. "I saw it. I mean, I saw that it wasn't there. And I saw Mad put it in there this morning."

"Me too," Lisa added, "we both did." The presence of the Assistant Headmaster seemed to scare her into using English.

Dr. Trent frowned at all of us. "I don't know what you and your friends are up to here, Madison, but if your laptop's no longer missing, this is not a matter for the administration to deal with." Then he turned to Turtell, who had been trying to slink away. "As for you, young man, you're not going anywhere."

As they headed down the hall, we could hear Stephanie telling Dr. Trent about the gender-neutral language policy again, and Dr. Trent snapping "I *know*!"

Turtell turned around and gave us a salute, then disappeared down the hallway.

I stared at my laptop again, then looked at my friends. "This is weird. I mean, it's weird, right?" I asked. "Who steals something, then returns it?"

Schuyler shrugged. "Considerate thieves?"

Lisa peered into my locker. "Are you both sure it was missing? I mean, maybe it was just under your gym clothes."

Were people under the impression that my gym clothes were particularly voluminous, or something?

"No," I said, "it wasn't there. We checked." I pulled my laptop out of my locker and looked at it. It looked okay — the hard drive and the battery were still both there. I put it in my canvas bag, and I looked around the rest of the locker for anything valuable.

Whoever this thief was — considerate or otherwise — I didn't want to give them the opportunity to steal anything else. There was nothing much else of value in the locker — I really didn't care if anyone stole my gym clothes. In fact, if they did get stolen, I would have an excuse not to attend gym, so that would be fine with me.

"Hey guys!" Ruth rushed up, looking out of breath, her normally sleek hair a little flyaway. "Sorry I'm late. Did we look at the profile yet?"

I'd almost forgotten that looking at Nate's profile was the whole reason I'd brought the laptop to school to begin with. "No," I said, "not yet —"

"Where were you?" Lisa asked, frowning at Ruth. "We had *une situation grave* here."

Ruth smoothed down her hair, looking worried. "What happened? I was taking my AP Physics test," she said with a groan, "and I don't know what I did — I think I spent too much time on the lab portion or something, because I didn't finish in time. I had to beg for fifteen extra minutes. And I still don't know if I passed."

"I'm sure you did great," Schuyler said encouragingly.

"I don't know," Ruth said, biting her lip. "I'll find out, I guess. Anyway, Mad — what happened with your laptop?"

Lisa and Shy filled her in, and Ruth listened quietly, not asking any questions until the end. "But why would they return it?" she finally asked, when they were through.

"Exactly!" Lisa said.

Schuyler frowned. "Could it have been Turtell?" she asked after a moment. "I mean, I know you're friends with him, Mad, but he *is* in the office a lot. And in detention a lot. And didn't Stephanie say they'd had some problems with locker thefts?"

I shook my head. "Turtell wouldn't steal from me." Ruth and Lisa raised their eyebrows at me. "He *wouldn't*," I insisted. "Turtell has my back. And if, for some reason, he did steal something from me, he certainly wouldn't return it."

The end-of-lunch bell rang, and I realized that none of us had eaten anything. "Guys, I'm sorry," I said. "None of you got lunch. I feel awful."

Lisa waved a hand impatiently at me. "*Bof*," she said. "We'll figure out who did this. *Je te* promise!"

221

The second bell rang, and Schuyler and Lisa headed to class with promises to "get to the bottom of this." But I didn't know what we were getting to the bottom of. The whole thing just left me feeling unsettled.

This must have been pretty obvious, because Ruth touched my sleeve and said, "Mad, are you okay?"

I rubbed my eyes. "I don't know," I said. My head was spinning as I tried to figure all of this out. Something had just happened, but I didn't understand what yet. Or why.

The final bell rang and Ruth bit her lip. "I'm happy to stay with you," she said, "but I have Spanish, and —"

"No, go on," I said. "*Vayas.*"

"Text me if anything happens."

"You got it." Ruth then gave me a quick hug and hurried down the hallway.

I had an open, which normally would have been cause for celebration, but right now I could have used a class, even English, to distract me from my own thoughts.

As the hallway cleared out, I took my lunch out to our rock, contemplating the situation as I walked. My contemplation (which may, admittedly, have veered into a brief fantasy of slow-dancing at the prom with someone who looked suspiciously like Nate) was interrupted by Connor, looking out of breath and staring up at me.

"Madison?" he called.

"Hey, Connor," I called down. "Come on up." I opened my laptop, preparing to check that everything was still on my computer and that nothing had been tampered with. I really didn't want to have to make an emergency trip to see Dell.

Connor hoisted himself up onto the flat surface of the rock, and I was glad for the opportunity to talk to him about his date tonight, and to subtly remind him that if he broke Schuyler's heart he'd have to answer to me. "What's up?" I asked, once he'd gotten settled.

"Bad news," he said gravely.

My jerk-dar immediately went up. "You're not canceling on Schuyler tonight, are you?" I asked him. "Because I know she's really looking forward to this, and —"

"No," he said. "Not that. It's your profile, Mad. It got hacked again."

CHAPTER 17

I sat on my bed, my laptop on my lap, staring at my
Friendverse profile. It was blank.

When Connor had told me I'd been hacked, it had
taken most of my inner resources not to hurl myself
backward off the rock.

After I'd stopped swearing — and frightening off the
random freshmen nearby, who were just trying to enjoy
their lunches — we'd gone to the library together. That
was where Connor had been spending his Independent
Study period doing Internet Liaison work for Dr. Trent.
When he'd seen my profile, he'd come looking for me.

"I thought you couldn't access Friendverse from the
school computers," I said, as I watched Connor log on.

He shook his head. "Who told you that?" he asked as
he brought up my profile from his buddy list.

I tried to remember, but the answer wasn't coming. We looked together at my profile, which had been last logged on to that morning — when I had most decidedly not logged on. It wasn't as damaging as last time — there were no comments propositioning my best friends' boyfriends, or spilled secrets or spelling mistakes — but in a way, it was almost as bad.

The profile was blank. Everything — all my interests, my comments, my music, my basic info — had been deleted. The only clue that the hacker had been there at all was the fact that my screen name had been changed to **Madison MacDonald SUCKS.** I felt like someone had slapped me.

"How could this have happened?" I asked, staring at the screen. "I mean, how could this have happened *again*?"

"Well," Connor said, taking out a notebook and pencil — clearly, he was taking his Internet Liaison responsibilities seriously — "has there been any unusual activity on your profile recently? An increase in profile views? Strange buddy invites?"

"No," I said, thinking. Then my stomach dropped. "But my laptop was stolen, then returned, this morning," I whispered. I shook my head. Someone had broken into my locker for the purpose of hacking me again? Seriously? "The hacker stole my laptop so they could hack me again, didn't they?"

It just made the hacking feel even more personal. Clearly, they weren't done yet — they still wanted to do *more* damage to my life. And the fact that they'd returned the laptop was chilling — it meant they cared more about hurting me than they did about making money by selling the pieces on the black market, or whatever.

"I think so," he said grimly. "If someone wanted to hack your profile again — and it seems that *is* what they wanted to do — and they couldn't figure out your password this time, they would have needed your laptop to do it."

I'd clutched my laptop to me little more tightly. "But how would that have helped?"

"Your password was probably stored somewhere on your computer," he said. "Frank Dell would probably be able to tell you more about it. But even if they couldn't find the information stored on your laptop, there are keystroke monitoring programs that can retrieve the most recent words you've typed."

And the last thing I'd written had been my Friendverse password, when I'd logged in before bed. I groaned, staring at the carnage in front of me.

"You should change your password," Connor said.

I nodded. He logged out and I logged in, changing my password to **OMGWTFSERIOUSLY??** as he looked the other way. I didn't feel up to putting in all my information *again*, but I did change the screen name to, simply, **Madison.** Then I logged out and stared at Connor bleakly.

He shook his head and gave a little laugh. "I guess you really pissed someone off," he said.

"Yeah," I said. But *who*? It wasn't Connor, it wasn't Kittson, it wasn't Travis, and it wasn't Sarah. Who had I made so angry that they would have done this to me, not once, but twice?

"At least we caught it early this time," he said, in the tone of someone who is determined to find the bright side. He and Schuyler really did have a lot in common, and I tried to shift my thoughts from my own baffling situation to their happier one.

"So what's the plan for tonight?" I asked, trying to smile.

As Connor and I walked back to the Student Center, he told me about the plan — dinner, a movie, coffee — which I assured him Schuyler would love. I also told him that her favorite flowers were Gerbera daisies, just in case he wanted to do anything with that information.

Then I went to my remaining classes with my head spinning. When I met up with my friends after classes were over, I decided not to tell them about the second hacking — if they saw my Friendverse before I'd had a chance to restore it, I could just tell them I was rethinking the layout or something.

But Ruth could clearly tell something was up; she was looking at me closely and kept asking me if everything was okay. I told her everything was. I'd talk to her about it later, alone. Schuyler and Lisa had entered into full-on Friday night mode, and I didn't want to harsh their vibe. Lisa had a date with Dave, and Schuyler had her date with Connor. Ruth was babysitting, and as everyone informed me of their plans, I realized I was the only one with nothing to do.

Of course. It was my first weekend back home without Justin as my boyfriend. I wondered what he and Kittson were doing tonight. Strangely, the thought of them together really didn't bother me all that much anymore.

But the fact that I was the dateless, planless loser who was sitting home alone really *was* bothering me. Even Travis had a date — before he'd gone out, he'd informed me that he, Olivia, and twelve other friends were going to the movies. This seemed to count, to Travis, as their first date.

My parents had invited me to go out with them and their Scrabble group, but I felt that I could only sink so low, and had refused.

So there I was on my bed with only my laptop for company.

I was just about to order some food and see what was on TV when the house phone rang.

I grabbed the extension, contemplating if I should just let the machine get it, when I saw the name on the display read ELLIS. My heart began to pound a little, and I answered.

"Hello?"

"Madison?"

There it was, that fantastic, slightly gravelly voice. I tried to remind myself to breathe, and that I was perfectly capable of forming complete sentences.

"Nate? I mean, hi, yes, it's Madison. So. What's up?" Well, so much for the "complete sentences" thing.

I could hear the smile in his voice when he spoke. "Are you busy tonight?" he asked.

****

"So this is a drive-in," I said, looking at the cars parked in rows across the field, and the huge screen set up at one end of it. We had paid for our tickets (well, Nate had paid and wouldn't let me pay my share, so I had insisted on getting the popcorn and drinks) and gotten our speaker when we had pulled in.

I was truly surprised to find myself there; Nate had refused to tell me where we were going, but had simply said to be ready to go in twenty minutes.

I'd immediately texted Ruth and Lisa, frantic. (I didn't want to interrupt Schuyler's date with Connor.) Lisa had been appalled that I would accept such a

229

last-minute date, but had been able to see past this and tell me to wear my jean mini and black V-neck. Dave had then commandeered her phone to tell me that he thought that was a hot outfit, and not to do anything he wouldn't do (winky face). Lisa had then told me that she and Dave had to have *"une petite conversation"* but to text her when anything — *anything* — happened. Or didn't happen.

I hadn't heard back from Ruth, but I figured she was already baby-sitting, and had more important things to worry about — like keeping small children alive.

But I kept my phone pulled slightly out of my purse, which was resting at my feet, so that I could see if I got a new text.

"This is a drive-in," Nate confirmed, taking a sip of his Coke. He raised an eyebrow at me, and I immediately felt jealous of his ability. "I thought you said on your Friendverse that you loved them."

I smiled at him. "Been looking at my profile, huh?"

"Well, you know," he said, placing the cup in the cup-holder. "Occasionally."

"I love the *idea* of drive-ins," I explained. "The fact that I've never been to one is beside the point."

"If you say so," he said with a smile. "Well, welcome to southern Connecticut's only drive-in."

We were in New Canaan, about to see an Audrey Hepburn double feature of *Charade* and *Wait Until*

Dark. We were sitting in Nate's surprisingly pimped-out red pickup truck, with the speaker hung over the driver's side window. The truck had a huge front seat with — my favorite feature — bench seats. Not that we were *going* to be making out or anything, but, you know, in case the possibility arose, bench seats just made it easier.

The thought of making out with Nate suddenly caused me to feel very warm, and I gulped down some Diet Coke.

"So," I said, once my temperature had been restored to something more like normal, "is this where you've seen all your obscure old movies?"

"You got me," he said. "*Charade*'s one of my favorites. I've never seen *Wait Until Dark*, though."

"I have," I said. "A few times."

Both of his (very cute) eyebrows went up. "Really?"

I liked being able to surprise him. "Really," I said. I explained that we'd done the play last year for our fall mainstage, so I'd watched the movie a lot for reference. "Remind me," I said, "to tell you the infamous Poison Jelly story."

"I'm going to hold you to that," he said.

It was beginning to get dark out; the first stars were starting to appear over the field, and I could hear the projector start up. A few moments later, the previews began. I pushed off my flip-flops and tucked my legs up under me. There was at least a person-space between me and Nate, but I was acutely aware of his proximity.

When Audrey Hepburn returned to find her Paris apartment empty, Nate moved a little closer to my side of the seat.

When she met Cary Grant for the second time, I shifted ever so slightly toward him under the ruse of reaching for my Diet Coke in the cupholder.

When Audrey and James Coburn were facing off in the phone booth, Nate rested his arm on the back of the bench seat, right above where my shoulders were.

When Audrey discovered who Cary Grant really was, and they started kissing as she repeated all his names, I moved close enough so that there was only room for a really, really small person between us.

There was a 20-minute break between the films, and I used it to get us some popcorn and send this text:

SENT 1 of 64
To: Lisa Feldman, Ruth Miller
Date: 4/11, 10:05 P.M.

OMG we're at the drive-in and he's thisclose to putting his arm around me. Two words: Bench. Seats. Wish me luck!!!

I got an immediate response back from Lisa.

From: Lisa Feldman
Date: 4/11, 10:07 P.M.
Go Mad!!! Tres bien! Justin who?

I smiled at that and turned my phone to vibrate. In actuality, I hadn't thought about Justin all night, with the exception of realizing that it was really nice to see a movie where things weren't blowing up all the time and people weren't naked for no reason.

By the time the second movie was about to start, it was completely dark out, and lightning bugs, the first of the season, were beginning to dart around. When I got back to the truck, I saw Nate standing next to it, taking pictures of the darkened screen.

"Hey," I said.

"Hey," he said with another of those contagious smiles. "That's a lot of popcorn," he said, gesturing to the tub I was carrying.

"Well, it's not a movie without popcorn." I nodded at the camera. "Giving into your weakness for things that are beautiful?" I asked.

"You got it." He closed his camera and put it back in his pocket. When we were both back in the truck, I noticed that Nate had slid almost to the center of the seat. I smiled, put the popcorn between us, and slid right next to him.

By the time Audrey Hepburn was vanquishing the murderer, his arm was firmly around my shoulders, and my head was resting on his shoulder.

****

"So," I said, as we drove through downtown Stanwich to Nate's favorite coffee shop, "I was playing the Audrey Hepburn part, and since the character is blind, every prop that was used had to be pre-set really carefully. Including the *knife* she uses to kill the murderer so the play can, you know, end."

"I think I see where this is going," Nate said.

We were driving, so we had our seat belts on (darn it) which limited how close together we could sit. But my legs were definitely swung over toward his side of the truck and there were definitely some *Omg are we going to kiss tonight?* butterflies in my stomach, which was both wonderful and excruciating.

"Right," I said, using all my willpower not to reach out and touch his hair. "So Rhiannon King was in charge of props, but on the closing night of the show, she had decided to make out with her girlfriend in the lightlock instead of pre-setting any of the props."

"Yikes," Nate said, pulling into a space in front of Stanwich Sandwich & Coffee and killing the engine.

"Exactly. So there I am, trying to be blind and kill Mark Rothmann, who was playing the murderer. But there was no knife there. And I seriously didn't know what to do."

"So what did you do?"

"Well, what anyone in that situation would do. I crawled over to the refrigerator, took out the jar of prop raspberry jelly, and started throwing handfuls of it at Mark, while I yelled, 'Poison jelly! Poison jelly!'"

Nate stared at me. "Then what?"

"Well, it took a minute, I guess because Mark didn't know the symptoms of jelly poisoning, but then he started flopping around, and then they brought down the lights and that was the end of the play."

Nate laughed, and then he just looked at me. "You know," he said, after a moment, "the first time I saw you on the boat, I knew you were going to be interesting. But you keep surprising me."

My heart started pounding again. "I do?" I asked, trying to keep my voice from squeaking.

"Yeah," he said. He looked at me intently and for a moment I was *sure* he was going to kiss me, but instead, he just tucked a stray piece of hair behind my ear, letting his hand rest on the bottom of the strand for just a second. "Coffee?" he asked, breaking away.

"Coffee," I agreed, trying not to be too disappointed.

We entered the coffee shop, and I couldn't help noticing our reflection in the glass window, and how good we looked together, how . . . well matched, in a weird sort of way. After I'd checked out the menu and decided on my latte flavor, my eyes wandered over the rest of the coffee-house. It was funkier and hipper than Stubbs, with a whole section of booths in the back. They were pretty filled up with couples and groups of kids and —

I looked closer. Sitting in a booth in the corner was Ruth.

I was shocked, and barely stammered out my order to the bored-looking barista. Had Ruth finished baby-sitting early? And what was she doing in Stanwich?

I looked over at her booth again, and saw that there was a messenger bag and a black hoodie on the seat across from her. So clearly, she was here with someone. But who was it?

And when had we started keeping secrets from one another?

I pulled my phone out of my purse and pressed speed dial #2 — #1 was voice mail — for Ruth. I was partially hidden behind a flyer-covered pillar, but when she answered, I planned on stepping out and surprising her. And while I was at it, maybe getting some answers.

I watched as Ruth heard her phone, pulled it out of her bag, and looked at the display.

Then she pressed a button to ignore the call and placed the phone back in her bag.

****

"Is everything okay?" Nate asked me for the third time.

"Fine," I said, trying to focus on what he was saying. "Fine. What — I mean, could you repeat that?"

Nate sighed, and I saw a flash of impatience cross his face. It was totally justified. After I'd suggested we get our coffee to go, he'd taken me to his favorite spot in Stanwich, a stone wall that overlooked the beach and water of Long Island Sound. Since it had gotten a little cold, I'd pulled on my sweater.

For the first time, I understood the appeal of the stone wall. We were sitting on it, kind of close to each other, holding our coffees and looking out over the water, which was gently lapping against the sand.

It was completely and utterly romantic. And yet, all I could think about was my best friend and whatever was going on with her.

"It's all right," he said, looking down at his cup and shaking it a little. "Maybe I should just take you home."

"Okay," I murmured, furious with myself. *Romantic setting! Cute guy!* But I just couldn't shake the image of Ruth looking at her phone, seeing my name, and choosing not to answer my call.

Nate drove me home in silence, and the harder I worked to think of something to say, the more impossible conversation seemed.

237

He pulled into my driveway, but didn't put the car in park, and didn't kill the engine. Clearly, there would be no making out tonight.

Darn it.

"Well, um, thanks," I said after a few moments of the two of us staring straight ahead at my house, sitting in silence except for the truck's rumbling.

"Sure," he said. "It was fun." The unspoken *until you just got weird and distant* hung palpably in the air between us.

"We'll talk soon?" I said hopefully.

"Absolutely," he said. He looked like he meant it, but he also looked confused and disappointed. He opened his mouth like he was going to say something else, but then he shook his head and closed it.

I felt the same way. "Night," I said finally. I smiled at him quickly, then got out of the truck.

Nate put the truck in reverse and backed down the driveway. Then he gave a quick, quiet honk and pulled away, down the street and out of sight.

CHAPTER 18

Song: Bewitched, Bothered and Bewildered/Ella
Fitzgerald
Quote: "The course of true love never did run
smooth." — Shakespeare

I slammed the door and trudged inside. My parents were sitting at the kitchen table, eating York minis and talking about their triple-word score. I grabbed a couple minis out of the bag and a CFDC (Caffeine-Free Diet Coke, a necessity if I was going to be drinking DC after midnight) from the fridge and told them good night.

I headed upstairs before they could ask me about my night, or tell me again about that time that my father got a 374 point word score on "whizbang."

The night, particularly the last half hour or so, kept replaying itself in my head. All the things I should have done — like not letting the Ruth sighting ruin my time with Nate — were suddenly becoming incredibly clear to me.

I got changed for bed, too tired to even text Lisa and give her a post mortem. And how would I deal with Ruth? Would I tell her that I'd seen her?

I was about to go to bed when I realized that my profile was still blank. Just as I would never go to bed without washing my face, I could *not* go to bed with an incomplete profile.

I gently grabbed my laptop, and logged on to Friendverse. The first thing I noticed, when I checked my friends' statuses, was that Nate had changed his screen name. He was now, simply, **Nate.** And he was currently online.

I saw that he'd also just updated his status.

Friendverse
Status Updates   See all

Nate is bewitched, bothered and bewildered
Updated 12:03 A.M.

Did that have something to do with me? It had to, right? I mean, it wasn't like he would have had time to be bewitched, bothered and/or bewildered by anyone else. He'd just dropped me off, after all.

I stared at his update, thinking. Then, realizing that he could now see that I was online, too, I updated my status as well. I took a cue from him and quoted the first line of the song's chorus.

Madison is wild again, beguiled again, a simpering, whimpering child again
Updated 12:04 A.M.

My eyes were glued to the status update page, waiting for something to happen. I knew that everyone else would be able to see my now slightly odd status, but I really didn't care. If Nate was trying to say something to me, I wanted him to know I was listening.

The update *ping!*ed.

Nate is a little bit skeptical.
Updated 12:08 A.M.

Okay, that definitely was a response to me. And not really a good one.

Heart pounding, I updated my status again.

Madison wishes he wouldn't be.
Updated 12:09 A.M.

His response was almost instantaneous.

Nate is just confused, then.
Updated 12:10 A.M.

Madison wishes she could have a do-over of the last half hour.
Updated 12:12 A.M.

241

Was that too forward? I barely had time to analyze, when his status changed again.

Nate is a big fan of the do-over.
Updated 12:13 A.M.

Was that a second-date invite? I couldn't really tell. I mean, we hadn't even been (technically) on a first date. According to the horrible book Lisa read last year, *The Rulez — For Teenz!*, a date had to be made at least three days in advance for it to be considered official. And while I didn't buy into that stuff, I appreciated the definitions.

Had it been a date? Was he asking me for a second one?

I decided to go noncommittal.

Madison is smiling.
Updated 12:15 A.M.

Nate is no longer bewildered or bothered.
Updated 12:16 A.M.

I stared at that last sentence again, realizing that he hadn't taken the "bewitched" part out of it. Which was him saying that he was "bewitched" by me. Bewitched! It was the most romantic thing that had ever happened to me.

242

Unless I was just reading too much into his status updates, which was entirely possible.

But I couldn't *quite* believe that.

I thought about just sending him the next song lyrics and really testing his musical theater knowledge, until I realized that the next lyrics talk about "worshipping the trousers that cling to him."

Somehow, I didn't think that would send the right message.

But I wanted him to know that I'd gotten what (I thought) he was trying to say.

Madison is twitching her nose.
Updated 12:18 A.M.

Nate is rolling his eyes.
Updated 12:19 A.M.

My update *ding!*ed again, and I saw that Lisa had changed her name and come online. Since all the updates were stored on the home page, she would only see my half. I could only imagine what she would think of them.

But at the moment, I really didn't care.

Lisse wishes that her boyfriend would air the pizza smell out of his car occasionally.
Updated 12:20 A.M.

Madison is doubting that Nate can twitch his nose.
Updated 12:21 A.M.

Lisse is wondering what Madison's been smoking.
Updated 12:22 A.M.

Lisse is also wondering why she didn't share.
Updated 12:22 A.M.

Nate is doubting there is such a thing as "poison jelly."
Updated 12:23 A.M.

Madison is thinking, "touché!"
Updated 12:24 A.M.

Lisse is very, very confused.
Updated 12:25 A.M.

Nate is going to bed.
Updated 12:26 A.M.

My heart sank a little when I saw that. While this wasn't the best way to flirt — after all, one of my best friends could see half of what was going on, even if she couldn't understand it — I didn't want this to end. And while I was glad we seemed to have erased some of the weirdness of the night, I wasn't sure that everything was okay.

Madison says "goodnight."
Updated 12:27 A.M.

Madison also says, "sleep tight." ☺
Updated 12:27 A.M.

Nate is smiling now.
Updated 12:28 A.M.

Nate has logged off.

I let out a breath as I watched Nate's online light fade to gray. I didn't know what things were, but they seemed better now.

I looked at my blank profile and thought that it actually wasn't so bad that way. It was a lot less cluttered, after all. I could just tell Schuyler and Lisa that I'd done some Friendverse feng shui. I smiled as I read through the chain of our updates. I really, really liked that it wouldn't make sense to anyone but Nate and I.

The update *ping*!ed.

Lisse is feeling tres out of the loop.
Updated 12:29 A.M.

Madison promises to tell her everything at breakfast tomorrow.
Updated 12:30 A.M.

Lisse likes that idea.
Updated 12:30 A.M.

Madison is thinking Stubbs at 11?
Updated 12:31 A.M.

Lisse thinks that sounds fantastique.
Updated 12:32 A.M.

Lisse est tres fatiguee — bonne nuit!
Updated 12:32 A.M.

Lisse has logged off.

I was glad that our breakfast had come about in this way; if Schuyler saw our updates, she would know what we were doing, and that she was welcome to come if she wanted to. But I had a feeling it was just going to be me and Lisa. And that sounded okay, surprisingly. I needed someone to talk to about the Ruth situation, and the person I would normally have talked to — Ruth — was not an option, for obvious reasons.

I updated my status one last time.

Madison is a SK.

Then, I examined my Top 8. After I'd been hacked, and as people had refriended me, I'd returned it to what it had been before. But it no longer seemed quite right.

I reorganized. Somehow, it felt really weird to still have Justin in my number one spot. And before I could lose my nerve, I pulled Connor and Sarah out and moved Nate up into the Top 8.

TOP 8:

RueRue

Lisse

Shy Time

Justin

pizzadude

ginger_snap

**Brian
(not Ed)
McMahon**

Nate

Then, smiling, I turned off my computer and went to bed.

CHAPTER 19

Song: I Hear The Bells/Mike Doughty
Quote: "It's discouraging to think how many people
are shocked by honesty and how few by deceit."
— Noel Coward

"So then what?" Lisa asked, leaning across the Stubbs table, eyes wide.

I had just described the date, and was now up to the weirdness of the Ruth sitch. "So then I called her, and she looked at the phone and didn't answer it," I said. I took a sip of my latte and smiled across the shop at Kevin. He'd given me lots of extra foam, just the way I liked it.

"*Incroyable*," Lisa murmured. "Well, the only reason she would ignore a call from *you* is if she was having some kind of romantic thing with someone." Lisa snapped her fingers. "I knew she had a crush on someone. I just knew it!"

"But then why didn't she tell us about it?" I asked, stealing a piece of Lisa's croissant. "She told me the other

248

night that she'd tell me as soon as she was ready. But if she's on a coffee date with someone, that sounds pretty serious, don't you think?"

"*Je ne sais pas*," Lisa said. She shrugged, but with both arms.

"Well," I said, brushing off my hands, "I suppose I'll just have to ask her tonight at Brian's party."

Lisa sat up very straight. "Party?" she asked, a glint coming into her eyes. "What party?"

****

"So he didn't kiss you?" I groaned. I was having some quality Schuyler time at her hair salon. Her stepmother made her get monthly lowlights, and Schuyler always got bored, so I usually went and hung out with her. Plus, I could usually get one of the stylists to give me a free bang trim.

"No," Schuyler said loudly above the sound of the dryer that was engulfing her head. "But it was a really great time anyway! Well, except for the movie part. Because it was subtitled, and I couldn't see anything. And Connor couldn't find his contacts or something, so neither of us really knew what was going on. Because neither of us speak Korean."

"But he didn't kiss you?" I said, looking sorrowfully out from under my overgrown bangs at a passing stylist.

"No," Schuyler said. "But he brought me Gerbera daisies, Mad! And you know those are my favorites! And we did hug good night."

"And?"

She sighed happily. "It was really great."

"Good!" I smiled at her. I was happy to hear her good news. While she'd been having her foils applied I'd filled her in on my semi-disastrous date and the Ruth weirdness. Shy thought that Ruth didn't know it was me who was calling and so had just ignored the call. I then told her that most people who aren't constantly tossing their cell phones out of windows usually take the time to program in their friends' numbers.

"Yeah," Schuyler said, shifting a little under the dryer. "I don't know when I'm going to see Connor next, though. I mean, aside from school on Monday. I mean *see* him see him —"

"You'll see him tonight, right?" I asked, completely without thinking. "At Brian's party?"

Beneath the dryer, Schuyler's eyes widened. "Party?" she asked hopefully.

****

In the backseat of Dave's BMW, I lowered my window. "God, Lisa was right," I said, breathing in the scent of the sweet, sweet fresh air. "Dave, please air out your car every now and then."

"Hey!" Dave said, catching my eye in the rearview mirror. "Who's giving you a ride?"

"Who told you about the party in the first place?" I retorted.

"Lisa," Dave said, pointing to the passenger seat, where Lisa was meticulously applying red lipstick, using the visor's mirror.

"*Oui*," Lisa said, barely opening her mouth as she concentrated on the task at hand. "*Bien sur.*"

"But who told *you*?" I asked her.

"*Bof*," Lisa said, waving a hand impatiently and placing the top back on her lipstick.

"I thought you said you put the pies in the trunk," I said. Dave had brought three cheese pizzas at my suggestion, in the hopes that Brian wouldn't notice I was bringing extra people with me. "It just really smells like garlic back here, Dave."

"Well, yeah," Dave said, seeing a yellow light in the distance and speeding up.

Driving with Dave was always interesting; it usually felt like some sort of spiritual experience, as I almost always found myself praying during some part of the ride. The fact that Lisa could apply makeup while he was driving was just a testament to how long they'd been together.

"I mean, I deliver pizzas," he continued. "And pizza fumes tend to linger."

"Tell me about it," Lisa muttered.

"What kind of pizza was this?" I asked, sticking my head a little farther out the window. "Entirely garlic and salami?"

"You'll never believe it," he said, "But last night I delivered another onion-anchovy-ham. I thought Ruth was the *only* person who would ever eat that."

"No," Lisa said, taking out her bronzer brush while I looked away, fearing for Dave's leather seats, "we delivered one about three weeks ago, remember? I still have the dry-cleaning bill, in case you don't."

"And you're sure it wasn't to Ruth?" I asked, joking.

"Not unless she moved to some big house on Lower Cross Lane," Dave said. He pulled onto the side of the road. "That's where both of them went, actually." He put the car into park. "And we're here."

We were actually still about half a mile from Brian's house, but since there was no crime in Putnam — except for mass embezzlement from the hedge funds, or whatever — the cops didn't have anything to do on the weekends except break up teenagers' parties. The clear giveaway that a party was going on was a lot of cars parked around one driveway. So by now, it was ingrained party etiquette for us to park a long way off and walk. The truly successful party could be judged by how far back the line of cars stretched.

Dave retrieved the pizzas from the trunk and we began the trek toward Brian's. I looked at him and saw that today's shirt featured a picture of our thirtieth president, and read *Keep It Coolidge!*

"So where is Schuyler?" Dave asked as we walked.

"She got a ride with Connor!" Lisa said excitedly. *"Oh, l'amour."*

"Brian is going to kill me," I said. "He told me not to tell anyone, and at least four extra people are going to be showing up at his 'study group' because of me."

"If he can't accommodate four extra people, his party is super lame," Dave said. "Plus, we brought pizza."

"And it's not like we don't know Brian," Lisa said, *"n'est-ce pas,* Mad? Mad?"

But I was no longer paying attention to what she was saying; I was transfixed by what I had just seen: a cherry-red, souped-up pickup truck parked along the side of the road.

****

We walked inside to find a typical Brian party going on. There were drinks and mixers in the kitchen, a blender whirring, and the contents of Mr. McMahon's liquor cabinet spread out over the kitchen island. I could see a keg on the deck and a cooler sitting next to it. I just hoped that somewhere in the kitchen, there was enough ice left for the Diet Coke I'd stashed in my purse.

253

For someone who said he didn't want to throw a raging party, Brian didn't seem to be trying very hard. The only concession he seemed to have made to the fact that he was grounded (and would probably be grounded again for most of the foreseeable future) was that he was insisting everyone take their shoes off at the front door.

When I'd come in with Lisa and Dave, Brian had frowned at me a little, but didn't seem overly mad, so I could relax on that front. I really didn't have much time to think about Brian anyway, as I was scanning the house for signs of Nate.

I didn't see him anywhere, but I did see Justin and Kittson over by the bookshelves in the living room, having what looked like an intense conversation. Kittson was wearing a tank top, and not sporting any hickeys that I could see, so maybe she'd finally gotten Justin to stop.

I saw Liz sitting by herself by the fireplace, staring out toward the patio where Jimmy was standing and looking a little wistful.

Ginger was outside, playing quarters with some people I didn't know, but who looked vaguely familiar from past Brian parties.

Connor and Schuyler were sitting on a couch in the TV room, and were looking incredibly cute together — I'd been right — but were also exuding the "early date and nobody else in the world exists right now" vibe. I wasn't even sure Schuyler was aware of where she was, as she didn't seem to be taking in any surroundings except for Connor. I'd go over and hang with them later, if I got the all-clear vibe.

When Dave and Lisa began making out on the couch in the living room (Dave and Lisa really couldn't resist couches. There wasn't much point in even trying to talk to them when there was a couch around. This was why I tried to go to coffeehouses with the two of them as infrequently as possible), I went in search of ice.

On my way to the kitchen I passed the study and I saw Turtell and Dell, standing across from each other. There was a weird vibe in the room, like I'd just interrupted an argument or something.

"Hey," I said, stopping in the doorway. Both guys looked my way. Neither looked too happy to see me. "What's up?" I asked, a little warily.

"Hello, Madison," Dell said, while looking at Turtell.

"Hey Mad," Turtell said. Then he crossed the room to stand next to me. "I need to talk to you," he added in a lower voice.

"Sure," I said. "Lay it on me. I'm just going to get a drink first."

"No," Turtell said, his voice dropping even lower. "I need to talk to you *alone*."

Oh *God*. Suddenly, all Turtell's weird, lingering looks made sense to me. When I'd told him to find a nice girl, had he thought I was talking about myself? I hoped he didn't have a crush on me. But why else would he want to talk to me *alone*? I never should have defended him back in fourth grade. My nine-year-old self's actions were coming back to haunt me. "Sure," I said, backing away a little. "Just let me get that drink first. Oh, and Dell," I said, remembering. "I need to talk to you about my laptop. There's been another issue."

"Oh?" Dell said, in his usual expressionless manner. He probably didn't want to say more than that, for fear I'd want a refund if there was something wrong with it. Which there was, but still.

"Yeah," I said. "I'll find you later. You too, Glen," I said, hurrying out of the room with the weird vibes. Hopefully I could avoid Turtell long enough for him to forget he wanted to tell me he had had a crush on me, and possibly for the past seven years.

I headed to the kitchen and grabbed a red plastic cup. I was even able to scrounge a few ice cubes, and I poured my Diet Coke into it.

I didn't really drink that much. After a party Brian had thrown last year — in which I'd discovered the dangerous siren song of Jägermeister, and then spent three straight hours throwing up, hearing snatches of conversation as Ruth and Lisa debated whether or not I needed to go to the emergency room — I'd pretty much put a kibosh on my consumption.

This had made me incredibly popular at parties, as people always wanted me to be their designated driver, so they wouldn't have to sleep on the party-thrower's living-room floor or have to deal with the judgmental looks from the straight-edge kids who ran SafeRides.

While I waited for my bubbles to die down so that I could pour some more, I looked through the kitchen window and saw Ruth standing out on the deck, talking to Jimmy. I looked around for Liz, but she was still by the fireplace. I really hoped the two of them would be able to work it out.

I watched Ruth talking intently to Jimmy, and wondered, again, what was going on with her. Had Jimmy been the one she'd been having coffee with — the one she had a crush on? I hoped not — anyone could see Jimmy wasn't going to be over Liz any time soon. And they belonged together, if only for the sake of the tattoos they'd both gotten over Christmas break.

As I watched Ruth lean in close to speak to him, I felt utterly at a loss. I hadn't talked to her at all today — I didn't know how to broach the ignored call. But I resolved to talk to her before the night was over. After all, this was *Ruth*. We could talk about anything.

"Madison MacDonald," a low, gravelly voice behind me said, "in the kitchen, with the Diet Coke."

I turned around and saw Nate there, holding a red cup of his own and smiling at me. He seemed to have

257

dressed up a little for the occasion, wearing a blazer over his jeans and T-shirt. He looked incredibly hand-some. I suddenly found myself wanting to do more than touch his hair — although I really wanted to do that, too.

But mostly, I was filled with the overwhelming desire to kiss him.

"Hey," I said. "Nate the Great." I smiled at him, hoped he had not suddenly developed the ability to read minds, and cursed myself for not taking a hint from Lisa and applying some lip gloss back in the car. Or on the 5K walk to the house. "Did you learn that from watching *Clue*, the movie?"

"I did indeed." He walked around the kitchen island to stand next to me. "Want to hit me with some of that stuff?" He was looking at my Diet Coke bottle.

"I don't know," I said, peering into his cup. "What was in there before?"

"Regular Coke."

"But I don't think you're supposed to mix them," I said gravely. I tapped my fingers on my chin. "I think there's some sort of rhyme. . . ."

Nate placed his cup down on the tabletop. "I said hit me."

"If you're sure," I said, and poured the remainder of the 20-oz. bottle into his cup. "Not so much with the drinking?" I asked lightly.

"Not tonight," he said, looking at me intently.

Thump, went my heart. "Oh," I said, trying to remember other words. I was sure there had to be some.

"Listen, Madison," he said. He took two steps closer to me and looked down into my eyes. Since Brian had made me take my shoes off and I was barefoot, he seemed even taller that usual.

"Yes?" I asked, trying to calm my heart, which had started going *thump-thump-thump*. I looked up into his gorgeous brown eyes and hoped my breath was okay, now that we were standing so much closer.

He took a deep breath. "There's something I've been wanting to ask you —"

"Madison!" Ginger yelled, stumbling into the kitchen and ruining the moment entirely. She stopped when she saw Nate. "Oh. Hi," she said. It looked like Ginger had been losing most of her games of quarters — or winning, depending on how you looked at it — as she was a little unsteady on her feet.

I gritted my teeth. What I wouldn't have given for Ginger to have stumbled in just two seconds later. What had Nate been about to ask me? I had an idea I maybe knew what it was, and *what if I was right?* Why couldn't Ginger have waited *two more seconds?*

"Hey Ginger," I said, trying to keep my voice as friendly as possible. "Um, this is Nate." I blushed a little when I said that. It made me feel like I was introducing

259

him because he was mine to introduce. Which was ridiculous, but still.

"Hey," Nate said, raising his eyebrows at me over his cup as he took a drink.

"Hey," she slurred. Ginger was one of the biggest lightweights I'd ever met, and at cast parties, someone (usually me) was always in charge of swapping her beer with nonalcoholic O'Doul's. But Ginger always seemed to think she got wasted anyway, so this technique did not seem to be solving the problem. "Madison," she said, walking up to me, swaying slightly, "I need to talk to you. *Alone.*"

I sighed. This seemed to be the theme of the party.

I didn't want to leave — Nate had been on the verge of asking me something important. And I really, really wanted to find out what it was. "Um, can we talk later?" I said, opening my eyes very wide at her on the last word, which Sober Ginger would have known meant, *Go away because I am talking to a cute guy.* Maybe it wasn't too late to salvage the moment.

Intoxicated Ginger, however, did not seem to speak that language. "No," she said, grabbing my arm, "I need to talk to you *now.*"

She pulled me out of the kitchen, and I glanced back at Nate, who looked like he was trying not to laugh, but also a little disappointed. "We'll talk later?" I called to him.

"Tewtally," he said with a smile. I noticed though, when he dropped his gaze, his expression became serious again, and he looked pensively into the cup.

Ginger pulled me out to the deck and sat down on the edge of one of the planters that ran along the perimeter.

"What's up?" I asked, settling in next to her. I was really trying not to be mad at her. She was drunk, after all, and probably had no idea that she'd just walked in on a potentially crucial moment.

I looked over Ginger's shoulder to see Ruth still talking to Jimmy. She didn't appear to see me, and I knew I'd have to go talk to her soon — I just hadn't decided what to do about the phone call thing.

Ginger blinked at me, tried to take a drink, then seemed to realize her cup was empty. "I need another beer," she slurred.

I had a feeling that this was not what she had wanted to talk to me about, that she'd probably forgotten what she wanted to talk to me about, and that her Rational Conversation Train had pulled out of the station a while ago. "Let me get you one," I said. I snagged an O'Doul's from the cooler and handed it to her.

"Oh, I like this one," she said as she squinted at the bottle.

"So, I should get back," I said after a few moments of silence, during which Ginger tried to peel off the label on her bottle.

She looked up at me and her eyes seemed to focus a little. "No!" she said, sloshing nonalcoholic beer on me. "Madison! I need to talk to you!"

"Sure," I said, as patiently as I could, wringing out my sleeve and hoping Nate was still in the kitchen, and still wanted to talk to me. "What is it?"

"Your hacker," she said, frowning with effort. "Here tonight — I heard them talking."

CHAPTER 20

Song: Hello, My Treacherous Friends/OK GO
Quote: "Everything happens to everybody sooner or later if there is time enough." — George Bernard Shaw

I sat up very straight. My heart had seemed to slow down when I heard Ginger say the words "hacker" and "here." I looked around, scanning the faces of the party-goers. "Who was it?" I asked Ginger. "You said they were here. *Who?*"

Ginger gulped her O'Doul's and blinked at me a few times. "Who's here?" she asked curiously.

"Pizza!" Dave said, coming out onto the patio, look-ing lipstick-stained and rumpled.

"Ooh, pizza!" Ginger said, sloshing more fake beer on me as she stumbled over toward where Dave had set up the pizzas on a patio table.

I sighed. "Ginger," I said, "I'll be right back, okay?"

"Sure," Ginger said vaguely, reaching for a slice and trying to eat it crust-end first.

I walked back inside the house, suddenly feeling very uncomfortable. The hacker was here? Here, in this house, at this party? And they'd been talking about me? *Who was it?*

I realized as I headed back to the kitchen that the only person I wanted to talk to about this was Nate. He'd probably have good advice for me, or would at least be able to help me sort through who it might be.

Because right now, I was literally clueless.

Nate wasn't in the kitchen, though, and I suppose I couldn't have expected him just to hang out while I tended to the whims of my drunk friend. I hoped he was finding people to talk to — I wasn't sure that he really knew anyone at the party except Brian.

Then I immediately amended this to hope that the people he was finding to talk to were guys. Or girls involved in very serious relationships.

I was tossing a few more ice cubes into my cup when Ruth walked into the kitchen.

"Hey," I said, surprised.

"Hey," she said, walking around the island to stand on the other side of me. "How's it going?"

"Not too bad," I said. "Except that Ginger said that my hacker was here, and talking about me."

Ruth looked around, just as I had done, as though expecting to see someone wearing a placard that announced their guilt, or a scarlet H, or something. "Here?" she asked.

I nodded. "Weird, right?"

She shrugged. "Maybe not. I mean, weren't there all those pictures from Brian's parties on your hacked profile? It makes sense that they might come back to another one."

"I guess," I said. "It's just creepy."

"Of course," she said sympathetically. Then she smiled at me. "I saw you talking to a very cute tall guy before," she said. "Was that Jonathan?"

"Nate," I corrected. "And yes. He's friends with Brian from a million years ago."

"Nate, right," she said, shaking her head. "And?"

I tried not to blush. Unfortunately, this is something that you have no control over whatsoever. "It's okay," I said. "It's good. I officially like him, I think."

Ruth raised her eyebrows at me. "What about Justin?" she asked.

I waved my hand, and as I did so, realized that I had picked up that gesture from Lisa. The next thing I knew, I'd be shrugging with one arm. I put my hand down. "That's over," I said, realizing as I said the words, how true it was. "Plus, he's with Kittson. And it's pretty perfect — the blond leading the blond."

"Huh," Ruth said, taking a sip from her red cup.

"So, what were you talking to Jimmy about before?" I asked, hoping this would lead to a conversation about who she'd been with last night and why she'd ignored my call. "I saw you guys on the patio."

"We were talking about Liz," Ruth said, shaking her head. "What else?"

"And?" I asked. "I can't get any info, because he still hates me. Are they getting back together?"

"He wants to," she said. "But I'm not sure it's going to work out."

"I hope so," I said, looking outside to see Jimmy eating a slice of pizza despondently.

"I'm not so sure," Ruth said, tipping her head in the direction of the living room, where Liz was now sitting on the couch with Dell, talking.

"No," I said, incredulous. "Liz and *Dell*?"

"Frank's a nice guy," Ruth said with a two-armed shrug. "She could probably do a lot worse."

"Or a lot better," I said, "like with Jimmy!" I could feel my voice rising, and I knew I was getting upset, but I really didn't care.

Of all the things the hacker had done, breaking up Jimmy and Liz had been the absolute worst. I was suddenly filled with rage. Whoever had done this to Jimmy and Liz was somewhere at the party, probably just doing a kegstand or playing beer pong without a care in the world. "Whoever did this," I said, shaking my head, "I just hate them so much."

"I know," she said, taking another drink. "I'm so sorry, Maddie."

"So I called you last night," I said slowly, deciding to just dive right in. "And you didn't answer."

"Yeah?" Ruth asked, looking maybe a little wary. "When?"

"Is there any more wine?" Kittson asked as she clomped into the kitchen in heels that made her as tall as me. This was no mean feat, as she was probably at least five inches shorter. Clearly, she had chosen to ignore Brian's "no shoes" edict.

"I didn't know there was wine," I said, looking around. "You can check the fridge."

"Bathroom," Ruth mouthed at me.

"Rue, wait —" I said, but she must not have heard me, as she continued out of the kitchen.

Kittson yanked the fridge open, grabbed a bottle of white from the door, uncorked it, and poured some into her cup. "So," she said, after sniffing the wine, swirling it around in her plastic cup, and finally taking a delicate sip, "I totally dumped Justin."

I was still looking where Ruth had disappeared, and I tried to switch my focus over to Kittson. "Really?" I asked. "Tonight? At ... a party?" I wasn't incredibly well-versed in dumping etiquette, but I had a feeling that might be frowned upon.

"Totally," she said, hopping up on the counter and kicking her heels against the trash compactor. "I was just like, no, you know? And he was all, let's give this another shot. And I was like, you wish. Plus," she said, taking another sip, "he's totally too short for my prom heels. I measured."

"Oh," I said, trying to process this information. "I'm sorry," I said after a moment.

Kittson shrugged. "Don't be. I can do so much better. In fact . . ." she said, leaning to the side, looking at someone who was passing the kitchen doorway. I turned around and saw Nate and Brian walking past. "Who is *that*?"

"Brian," I said, hoping she wasn't talking about Nate. "This is his house."

"Not Brian," she said, rolling her eyes at me. "The tall emo hottie."

"He's not emo," I said heatedly. "I mean, he's wearing a blazer, for God's sake. Anyway, that's Nate."

"Oh yeah?" she asked, leaning over again so far that she was practically lying on the counter. "He's cute."

I got so jealous when she spoke these words, it was like the world turned green for a second. "He," I said, when I could trust myself to speak again, "I mean, he and I — we're kind of —" I wasn't even sure if I could be saying this. But we *were* kind of, weren't we?

Kittson held up her hands. "Say no more," she said. She arched an eyebrow at me. "So how long have you two been . . . ?"

"Oh," I stammered. "I mean we're not yet offi-cially . . . that is, I mean . . ."

"Then why are you in here talking to me?" Kittson asked, as she hopped off the counter, slung her purse down from her shoulder and stood in front of me.

"Kittson, what —" I said as she unzipped a formida-ble makeup case, unscrewed the top of a small gold tube, squirted some clear liquid into her palms, and ran her hands through my hair.

"Better," she said, whipping out a lip gloss and apply-ing it with such speed I didn't even have the chance to see what color it was. "Close," she said, and I figured it would be easier to obey her, so I closed my eyes. As I stood there and she smoothed something onto my eyelids, I thought how bizarre it was that Kittson Pearson was giv-ing me a makeover. Not bad bizarre, just surprising. And that it might not have happened at all if I hadn't been hacked. Strange but true.

After a few moments, she stood back to admire her handiwork. "*So* much better," she said, and I tried not to feel insulted. "Now go flirt with him."

"Okay," I said, heading out of the kitchen. I stopped at the doorway and turned around to see her sipping wine and checking out the prospects in the backyard. "Thanks," I said.

"De nada," she said airily.

I headed out into the living room, looking for Nate, and still keeping an eye out for anyone who looked like a potential hacker. I saw Schuyler and Connor, sitting closer together than ever. Shy came out of her reverie long enough to smile and wave at me, then turned back to Connor. Liz was still talking to Dell on the couch, and I could see Jimmy on the other side of the room, staring at them and looking livid. But no Nate.

I was heading into the TV room to see if I could find him when someone grabbed my arm, yanked me into the study, and shut the door.

CHAPTER 21

Song: Taken Aback/The Rocket Summer
Quote: "You observe, but you do not see."
— Sherlock Holmes

I whirled around to see Turtell standing in front of the door, looking uncomfortable. He let go of my arm and stuck his hands in his pockets. "Glen!" I said. "What are you doing?"

"I told you I had to talk to you, Mad," he said. "And that I had to talk to you alone."

"Oh, right," I said. With everything that had been going on tonight, I'd forgotten about his crush. I tried to think how to let him down easy, and wished that Kittson hadn't given me a makeover. It was probably just making this harder for him. "Listen, Glen," I said as kindly as possible, "you know I like you as a friend. And I really think we should stay *friends*. It's just easier that way, and —"

271

"Madison, what are you talking about?" he said. "Listen, I need to talk to you about your computer."

"Oh," I said, trying not to feel disappointed. But this was the second guy in four days who hadn't actually been hitting on me when I'd thought he had. It was getting a little demoralizing. "Well, what about it?"

"Listen," he said. "You know I'm in the office a lot."

"I'm aware," I assured him.

"So I've had access to certain things — to seeing certain things. And when you have that kind of information, it's hard to know what to do with it, you know?"

"Glen," I said slowly, taking a step back from him, "what are you saying?" I suddenly remembered all the miraculously returned Metallica CDs, and how he seemed to get so anxious whenever anyone talked about the locker thefts.

"I'm saying," he said, running a hand through his hair and looking frustrated, "that I probably should have told you this before. And I'm sorry. But the database of locker combinations, Dr. Trent's database —"

The door swung open then, and Kittson stood on the other side, looking surprised to see me.

"Madison," she said, frowning at me. "What are you doing here?"

"Kittson," I said, wishing that people would just stop walking into rooms I was in, "I'm kind of in the middle of something here."

"Yes, but why?" she asked, glancing at Turtell, then double-taking and looking back at him for a long moment. "I mean, he's not that Nate guy."

"No," I said, "but we were in the middle of a conversation, so —"

"That's okay, Mad," said Turtell, whose eyes hadn't left Kittson since she entered the room. "I can find you later."

"I thought you said it was important," I said, frustrated.

"It's okay," he said, placing a hand above Kittson's head and leaning against the doorframe, "I'll catch you later."

"You're Glen, right?" Kittson asked, running a hand over her bangs. "The one who's always getting suspended?"

Turtell looked down modestly. "I don't know," he said. I noticed that his voice was suddenly about an octave deeper. "Sometimes I just can't help myself."

"I know what you mean, Glen," Kittson purred.

I was suddenly feeling very in the way, and also a little surprised at Kittson's audacity. I mean, she'd only been single for forty-five minutes, *tops*. Still, I couldn't help but admire her directness.

"I'm going to go," I said. Neither of them were paying any attention to me anymore, and I sighed and squeezed past them in the doorway. The door shut behind me almost immediately.

What had Turtell been about to say? Had he been the one who'd stolen my laptop? It certainly sounded that way, but somehow I just couldn't believe it. But had he *known* who had done it? Cursing Kittson and her distracting ways, I went in search of Nate, so we could finally finish our conversation.

After giving a quick survey of the main rooms — which were looking distinctly worse for wear — and not seeing him, I moved into the back section of the house, and had just stepped into the mudroom and turned on the light when I realized I wasn't alone.

Justin was in there, sitting on the cushion-covered bench.

"Hey Justin," I said, backing out of the room. He probably wanted some time to mourn the loss of his relationship. I was half-tempted to tell him to avoid the study, but figured he would just have to learn that on his own. "Sorry," I said, turning to go.

"No, Madison, wait," Justin said, standing up and walking towards me. "I want to talk to you. I've been looking for you."

I looked around. "No, you haven't," I said. "You were sitting here in the dark."

"But I *wanted* to look for you."

I was on the verge of telling him that this was not at all the same thing, when he took a step closer.

"Madison," he said, "I think that it was a mistake for us to break up. I mean, don't you? I've really missed you," he said, leaning even closer.

Shocked, I took a step back. "Justin," I said, "what are you talking about? That isn't even true. I know that Kittson just broke up with you."

"I broke up with her," he said earnestly.

I was not quite able to prevent myself from rolling my eyes.

"I did," he insisted. "Things haven't been right between Kittson and me for a while. I just missed you, Mad. And since you never really wanted to break up with me in the first place, it makes sense to get back together, right?" He looked at me expectantly.

I was silent, trying to think about all of this. "So," Justin continued, "to make a long story short —"

"Too late," I said automatically.

"What?" he asked. He stared at me blankly. "What are you talking about?"

"Nothing," I said. "You wouldn't understand." I looked at his cute, entirely bland face and realized this was true. How could I ever had thought he was my tortoise? We didn't even have anything in common. "Look, Justin," I said, "I think we should just —"

I had been about to say "call it quits" or "call it a day."

But I didn't get the chance, because in that moment, Justin took another step toward me and kissed me.

I immediately tried to get away, but Justin was being particularly enthusiastic with his kissing, and this made it a little difficult. Finally, I pushed him away and stepped back.

Which was when I saw Nate standing in the mudroom doorway, staring at me with a shocked expression.

He only stood there a second before turning and walking away.

"Nate!" I called, starting to follow him, but Justin grabbed my hand.

"Where are you going, Maddie?" he asked, a dopey expression on his face. "We were just getting started, right?"

"Justin," I said, yanking my arm free, "we're not getting back together."

"We're not?" he asked, looking crestfallen.

"No," I said, then realized he'd just been dumped twice in one night. "Um, sorry." With that, I ran out of the mudroom, looking around for Nate. I had to tell him that that hadn't been what it *really* must have looked like.

The front door had been left ajar and I ran out, to see a tall figure walking down Brian's driveway.

"Nate!" I yelled, starting to run after him. But Brian had a gravel driveway, and I knew I wouldn't get more than three steps without my shoes. Cursing Justin, and Brian and his stupid shoe idea, I grabbed the first pair of flip-flops that looked like they'd fit me. Then I ran down the driveway and into the street, just in time to see the taillights of a red pickup truck disappearing down the street.

Nate was gone.

****

I was sitting on the top front step half an hour later, trying to figure out what to do. I had to tell Nate the truth, obviously. That I hadn't been making out with Justin; I'd been kissed against my will. But would he believe me? And after what he'd seen, would he even want to?

"Heyyyy Mad," Ginger said, stumbling up to me and sitting down next to me on the step. "Howzit going?"

"Okay," I said, lying through my teeth. "How are you?"

"Tired," she said, her head lolling dangerously close to my shoulder. Once Ginger passed out, she became almost impossible to move. This was why, at last year's *Willy!* cast party, we'd had to let her sleep off her O'Doul's on a trampoline in Mark's backyard.

I sighed. "Go find your keys," I said, standing up and pulling Ginger to her feet. "I'll drive you home."

CHAPTER 22

Song: Putting It Together/Stephen Sondheim
Quote: "All other things being equal, the simplest solution is the best." — Occam's Razor

It was 3 A.M., again, and I was awake. Again.

My mind was swirling with everything that had happened at the party — with Nate, with Justin, with Ruth, with Kittson and Turtell. It was all adding up to something, but I couldn't seem to quite get my head around it. And normally I was pretty good at math.

I turned on my bedside light, got out of bed, and walked over to my window. My parents had been asleep when I'd come in, and I hoped I could get up early enough so that I could drive Ginger's car back to her before they'd start asking pesky questions about the strange SUV parked in their turnaround. I pushed open the window, leaned my elbows on the sill, and breathed in, trying to clear my head.

Then I walked over to my cork wall, looking at the pictures I had pinned to it.

Me. Lisa. Dave. Justin. Schuyler. Connor. Jimmy and Liz. Ruth. Ginger. Sarah. Brian. Turtell. Kittson. Dell.

I pulled them down, one by one, feeling like I needed to get my thoughts up on the wall where I could see them. I took out the list Ruth had made for me a week ago, when all this had begun, and pinned it to the center.

Then I started putting up pictures in different corners, trying to figure out people's agendas and wants and feelings. Trying to work through the time line of everything that had happened. When I was done, I stepped back and stared at it for a minute. It still didn't make any sense.

Then I wrote on notecards the three things I still had lingering questions about, and pinned them to the board.

Pizza/Lower Cross Lane
Jonathan
Q

Then, feeling like I was getting a little closer to the answer — whatever it might end up being — I went to bed.

But I didn't go to sleep for a long, long time.

****

"Where are we?" Ginger asked, blinking unhappily in the bright sunlight.

"We're going to my house," I said for the fourth time in what was only a mile-long drive. "Now make a left up here." I'd gone over to Ginger's as soon as I had woken up, to try and make the car switch before my parents noticed her car. I had done this often enough after parties to know the routine, but that didn't make it any less nerve-wracking.

"Here?"

"Yes," I said, "and it's the third house on the right."

Ginger pulled into the driveway a little more sharply than I would have advised, and parked in the turn-around. "Thanks," I said. I studied her closely. She was looking pretty rough. "Are you going to be able to get home okay?" I asked her. "Do you need me to GPS your house?"

"I'll be okay," she said, drinking from the bottle of water I'd brought her when I'd gone to her house. "But, um, I needed to ask you something, Mad."

"Shoot," I said, casting a glance toward my house, and hoping my parents weren't up and about yet.

"Did you . . . I mean . . ." Ginger rubbed her hand over her eyes. "Marilee told me that one of the blogs that got sent out when you were hacked . . . you said that I was annoying and chatty and a lightweight." She looked at me, her eyes red. "Did you say that about me, Mad? I thought we were friends. I mean, I know the lightweight thing is true, but the other stuff?"

"Well, not exactly," I said, almost by rote now. "I mean, I never would have written it, and certainly never put it online, there's a difference. . . ."

Then I looked at Ginger, and saw how hurt and surprised she seemed even in her hungover state. And I realized that I'd gotten it wrong from the beginning. There *wasn't* a difference, after all. "Yes," I said slowly. "I did say those things. And I'm really, really sorry, Ginger."

She blinked at me. "Oh," she said. "Well . . . okay."

"Okay?" I asked, surprised.

"Yeah," she said. "I mean, just don't say it again though, okay, Mad? Or if you do, say it to me."

I smiled at her, incredibly relieved. "You got it."

****

"Dad," I said, walking into the kitchen, surprised to see him there. I'd kind of been hoping I could sneak in on little cat feet before anyone noticed I'd been gone.

My father looked up from where he was sitting at the kitchen table, staring at the Scrabble board. He looked surprised to see me as well. "Where did you come from?" he asked. "I thought you were upstairs sleeping."

"Getting coffee," I said. I then realized I wasn't holding anything. "That . . . I drank already."

"Oh," my father said, turning back to his board.

I took a seat across from him at the table and looked at all the empty squares and tiles. "I don't get why you and Mom are so obsessed with this game."

"Well," my father said, eyes going between his tiles and the board, "it's a puzzle. And most of the time, the answer you need is sitting right in front of you, if you can only see it."

A faint bell started ringing in my head.

"Huh," I said. I stared down at his board again. "Go here," I said, tapping a freestanding *T* that could be filled in.

"No, no," he said, eyes on his tiles. "You want words that are going to intersect. You're not going to get very far if you're using words on their own. They're stronger if you can get them to work together."

The bell was getting a little louder.

"Interesting," I said. I watched as my father stared at the board, wishing I'd gotten some real coffee, not just alibi coffee. "That's not a word," I said when he put down OCCAM.

"Sure it is," he said, making a note on his paper. "Fourteenth-century monk." I sighed, sensing my dad going into trivia mode. "He coined Occam's Razor: 'The simplest solution is usually the best.' Or something like that."

The answer was in front of me . . . if only I could see it. Things are stronger when they work together. The simplest solution is usually the best.

The bell in my head suddenly got very loud, and I felt myself on the verge of the answer. "Thanks, Dad," I said, dashing upstairs.

I walked to the corkboard, looking at everyone who was up there, and all their different and potential motives.

And just like that, I saw the answer.

I couldn't believe it, but the pieces were all falling into place.

It was only half the story, though. I grabbed my phone, scrolled through my contacts, and called a number. We had a brief conversation, and verified what I'd had a lingering question about.

Then I looked up an address on Lower Cross Lane, just to make sure. It was correct. It was all coming together, even if the answer was breaking my heart. I'd been betrayed by someone I'd thought would always have my back.

I took a deep breath and made three phone calls, two to the people who had done it and one for moral support. I said the same thing in each one.

"Hey," I said, three times, "I need to talk to you about something. Can you meet me in Putnam Park in twenty minutes?"

CHAPTER 23

Song: No, It Isn't/+44
Quote: "You must seek the truth within — not
without." — Hercule Poirot

Putnam Park was one of the smaller parks in town, but it had always been my favorite. It had shaded paths surrounding a wide, open expanse of green and a small pond that always held ducks, and occasionally swans. There were benches on the perimeter of the pond that were excellent for duck-watching on nice days. I put my phone in my pocket, took a deep breath, and walked over to the benches.

Ruth was there, waiting.

"Hey," I said. "Have you been waiting long?"

"No," she said. She stood up, playing with her "R" necklace, which was visible below the scarf she had wound around her neck. "What's up?"

I took a deep breath. "I figured out who did it," I said. I looked around the park, which was empty except for a few senior citizen power walkers who were doing loops around the pond. "Who hacked me."

"Really?" Ruth said, sliding her "R" back and forth. "That's great! Who was it?"

"They're coming," I said. We stood in silence for a second. "I remember the first time I came here," I said. "It was in third grade, I think. Carrie Tolliver had her birthday party by the pond and people kept trying to feed cake to the ducks. Remember?"

Ruth adjusted her scarf. "No," she said. "I wasn't invited."

I tried to cast my mind back eight years. "Really?" I said. "I could have sworn —"

"No," she said. "I had been really good friends with Carrie, but as soon as you moved here, that was all over. I remember," she said with a small laugh, "what it was like when you came. You were from *Boston*! And you wore all these amazing clothes from Gap Kids. Like, whole matching outfits. And everyone just fell all over themselves to be friends with you."

I stared at Ruth levelly. "I didn't know any of that," I said. "I was just so happy to meet you — to have a best friend."

"Me too," Ruth said, after a moment. "Of course."

I looked across the park. "They're here," I said.

Just a little late, Dell and Turtell were entering the park from opposite sides and walking toward us.

"Is that Turtell?" Ruth asked. "And Dell?"

I sighed. "I'm afraid so."

The guys were looking at each other warily. I couldn't help notice that even though he looked apprehensive, Turtell also looked very happy, and I guessed that things had gone well with Kittson last night.

"What's this about, Madison?" Dell asked when they reached us. "I don't have time to be hanging out in parks. I have work to do."

"I'm sure you do," I said evenly, staring at him. He stopped protesting.

"Seriously, Mad?" Turtell said. "I'm happy to hang whenever — that is, if Kittson says it's okay — but what are we all doing here?"

"We're here because my Friendverse got hacked," I said. "Because someone set out to hurt me and wreck my life — and not only mine, but other peoples', too. To break up me and my boyfriend. To break up a long-standing couple. To possibly jeopardize my position in student government and turn my friends against me. I know who did it. And I think I know why. And that's why we're here."

Dell opened his mouth to protest.

"Dell," I said, "you hacked me."

Dell closed his mouth.

"When you repaired my computer, you got my Friendverse password off it. You were able to hack into my account with no problem because you knew the password. You also knew the letter Q wasn't working, which is why no Qs showed up in the hacked profile, and you were the only one who knew that."

Dell was staring at me, his face growing red.

"When you set up the locker combination database for Dr. Trent, you kept a copy for yourself. That's how you were able to open my locker when I was in class, take my laptop out of it, and then return it again. I wasn't supposed to get out of class early, so I wasn't supposed to have known this. But I found out. And when you stole my computer, you got my password off it to hack me again. Luckily, I changed my password again before major damage could be done."

Dell's face was incredibly red now. He looked both embarrassed and angry, but still wasn't saying anything.

"Did I get something wrong?" I asked. "I can understand how you did all those things — I just can't understand why you'd have *wanted* to. You have means and intent. But you're missing motive."

"Um, Mad," Turtell said, "I really don't understand why I'm here."

"Oh, you're just here for moral support, Glen," I said. Then I turned to Ruth. "So why'd you do it?"

CHAPTER 24

Song: Yes It Is/The Beatles
Quote: "Isn't it nice to know a lot? And a little bit not."
— Into the Woods

Ruth blinked at me and laughed. "What are you talking about?" she asked. "I don't know what you're talking about."

I stared at her. I felt a tiny flicker of hope that maybe, just maybe, I'd gotten all this wrong. But deep down, I knew it wasn't the case, as much as I might want it to be.

"Really?" I asked, trying to keep my voice level. "You had nothing to do with my hacking?"

Ruth looked directly at me. "Maddie, of course not. You're my best friend."

"Aren't you hot?" I asked. "It's getting warm out."

Ruth looked down at her scarf and adjusted it, and as she did so, I saw a bright-red hickey on her neck. It was all the remaining proof I needed.

"You got Dell to hack me," I said, knowing I had to go forward with this. "You masterminded this whole thing. And don't call me Maddie."

"What are you *talking* about?"

"Are you seriously going to deny it?" I asked. Ruth crossed her arms over her chest and stared at me.

"Fine," I said. "I can't believe I have to do this," I said, staring at the person I'd believed to be my best friend, and telling myself not to cry until I got through it.

"So," I said, trying to keep my voice from shaking, "you were my best friend."

Ruth flinched at the use of the past tense.

"You knew everything about me. You knew I was going away on spring break, and that there wouldn't be any real internet on the ship. You had enough pictures from parties we'd been to together to fake a horrible profile. You knew all those secrets so you could blog about them. And you broke up me and Justin because you wanted to go out with him."

Ruth's hand immediately flew to her neck.

"I assume that's from when you hooked up last night?" I asked. She stared at me, stony-faced. "I hope you also know that he asked me to go out with him again before that and I turned him down."

"He mentioned it," Ruth spat.

"You've had a crush on him for months," I said. "You first started crushing on him when you were tutoring him, right?" I asked. "Kittson knew about you — not who you were, but just that Justin was stringing along some girl. But when he started going out with me, you had to break us up."

"Oh, it was more than that," Ruth said angrily. "You didn't even appreciate Justin. You never did. You just thought he was cute — you never saw what was there."

"And you did?" I shot back.

Turtell and Dell were looking back and forth between the two of us, as though we were the tennis ball in a particularly violent match point at the US Open.

"I did," she said.

"But it didn't work," I said. "Even after you hacked me to break up with him, he still chose Kittson."

"You think that's the only reason?" Ruth asked with a short laugh. "You think that's the only reason I had Dell hack you? I was so tired of all of it — so tired of everyone buying into the Madison MacDonald myth. I was *sick* of it. I've been dealing with it since third grade."

"What do you mean?" I whispered. I could handle this when I thought it had been about a boy. I didn't know if I could handle the way my "best friend" was looking at me at the moment.

"Oh," Ruth said, her voice rising, "the fact that everyone thinks you're *so* nice and *so* sweet, when all you do is talk about people behind their backs. I didn't write

290

anything that you hadn't said, Madison. I just thought that people should know what you'd been saying about them. And I just wanted people to see that you weren't this great, wonderful person. Do you know what it's like to be *your* best friend? To have to listen to you complain about your boyfriend not paying enough attention to you, or the fact you have so many lines to learn for your lead in the play, or the fact that your parents are taking you to *Ecuador* for spring break?"

Ruth stared at me hard. "Do you know how tired I am of being in your shadow? You've been doing it our whole friendship," she said, her voice breaking. "And I can't take it anymore."

I was crying now; I couldn't help it. Turtell fished in his pockets and handed me a very grungy-looking tissue. "Thanks," I said, trying to use the one clean corner.

"Are we done here?" Dell asked, looking uncomfortable.

"Not yet," I said, trying to pull myself together. "Not quite yet." I blew my nose and took a breath. "It was the breakup of Jimmy and Liz that had me puzzled. Why would whoever hacked me care about breaking them up? I didn't understand it until last night."

I looked at Dell. "You had a crush on Liz, right?" I said. Dell's face, which had just about returned to its normal pasty shade, was going red again. "She's in your AP

Physics class, and you fixed her computer for her in March. But you didn't really fix it at all. You kept making tweaks to it so she'd have to come back. And since Ruth is terrible with computers, she couldn't hack me on her own. So when she came to you for help, you had a reason to do it — to break up Jimmy and Liz so you could go out with her."

Dell still wasn't saying anything. He just stared at me, impassive, almost bored.

"What I can't believe, though, is that you would have sold out Glen. You had your copy of the locker combinations and have been stealing things out of people's lockers, and then hinting that Glen here might have had something to do with it, knowing that Dr. Trent would never suspect you."

"So?" Dell asked, smirking. "So what? So I hacked you, Madison. And Dr. Trent's too much of an idiot not to realize that of course I was going to keep a copy of the locker combinations. But you're never going to prove any of this. I hope you've had fun playing Veronica Mars. But now I have to go."

"Not yet," I said, pulling my phone out of my pocket. "Did you get that, Connor?" I asked.

"Yeah," Connor said on the other end, sounding stunned. "*Jesus*, Mad."

"I know," I said. "And you recorded it for Dr. Trent?"

"Every word," he said.

"Thanks, Connor," I said. "I appreciate it." I dropped my phone back in my pocket. Dell had now turned white, and Ruth was staring at me open-mouthed. "Sorry," I said. "But you can't do that to people and get away with it."

"Dude," Turtell said, giving me a fist bump. "Nice."

"What is he even doing here?" Ruth snapped.

"Glen was instrumental," I said. "He'd been able to witness Dell coming and going from Dr. Trent's office, and was able to overhear enough so that he could guess that Dell had no intention of ever destroying the locker combination database and in fact, fully intended to let Glen take the blame."

"You got it," Turtell said. "Sorry I couldn't tell you that last night. But I got, um, distracted."

"It's okay," I said. "You told me this morning."

"Gotta bounce," Turtell said. "Good luck with . . . all this. Oh, and Kittson wants you to call her."

"Okay," I said. "Thanks, Glen."

Turtell walked across the field, hopping the low stone wall rather than opening the gate.

I turned back to Dell and Ruth, who were arguing.

"You promised me," Dell said in a low, angry voice, "that nothing would happen. My academic career is on the line —"

"I didn't know this would happen," Ruth cried, cheeks flushed. "I didn't think she'd figure it out!"

293

"Sorry to let you down," I said.

"I'm leaving," Dell said, glaring at both of us. "I don't think I should say anything else."

"Just FYI, Liz is going out with Jimmy again," I said before he could walk away. "Sorry. But they activated their joint Friendverse account this morning, and both their statuses say 'Taken.'"

I saw Dell's face fall before his usual impassive expression returned. Then he turned around and stalked out of the park.

It was just Ruth and me now. Exhausted by all of this, I sat down on the nearest bench. To my surprise, she sat down as well, on the opposite end.

"How'd you figure it out?" she asked after a moment. "That it was me?"

"It wasn't easy," I said with a sigh. "You did a really good job. But there were clues. You were the one who sent me on a wild goose chase of people who had nothing to do with this. You had your pizza delivered to Dell's house on Lower Cross Lane — I Googled the address — twice, back when you were hacking me during spring break, and then on Friday night, while I assumed the two of you were planning for the party. I saw you with someone at Stanwich Sandwich — someone who wore a black hoodie — Dell. And you were talking to Jimmy at the party, trying to convince him it was totally over, right? While Dell was putting the moves on Liz."

294

"Yes," Ruth said, sounding exhausted. "You got it."

"But what really tipped the scales happened last night. You called Nate 'Jonathan.' I'd never called him that, but it was the name in my second password."

"Yeah," she said. She slumped back against the bench. "What's happening with that, anyway?"

Out of habit, I was about to tell her all the details. But then I realized she wasn't my best friend anymore. And if she'd been feeling this way for as long as she said, she probably hadn't been my best friend for a while. "It's a WIP," I said finally, and she gave me a sad smile and stood up.

"I better go," she said. She looked as shaken as I felt. I looked up at her and knew our friendship was over. It had broken, right there in the park. "Talk to you later?" she asked.

I couldn't fill in my response. It just didn't feel right. "Yeah," I said sadly.

Ruth seemed to realize this, and after a moment, she nodded and walked away, her shoulders hunched.

****

I cried on the bench for sixteen minutes, according to the clock on my cell phone. But then, with the help of Turtell's tissue, I attempted to pull myself together.

I had a boy to talk to. And I had a bulletin to send.

295

CHAPTER 25

Song: Wouldn't It Be Nice?/The Beach Boys
Quote: "Try to reason about love, and you will lose
your reason." — Anton Chekhov

Friendverse Bulletin
From: Madison
To: All friends
Sent: 4/13, 12:05 P.M.

Hey everyone. As I'm sure you all know, my Friendverse profile was hacked over spring break. The hackers set out to do a lot of damage to my life, and to your lives. I'm writing now to apologize to anyone who was hurt by this hacking, and to take responsibility.

The hackers were discovered today, and I hope they'll be dealt with by the school administration. But it was actually due to my actions that you were hurt, and I wanted to apologize. What the hackers wrote about you on my profile, or in bulletins and blogs were things I had said in the past, behind your backs. I never should have said these things. And if I was going to

296

say them, I should have had the courage and decency to say them to your faces.

I regret this, and I'm truly sorry for any hurt I may have caused you.

And I promise, in the future, not to reveal your secrets, talk about you behind your back, spill your illicit hookups, or make fun of your eyeliner application.

And don't worry, my new password's encrypted.

I hope we're all still friends.

Love,
Mad

I finished typing this bulletin on my phone and, thumbs aching, pressed **SEND.** I watched the e-mail icon disappear, off to my friends' Friendverse inboxes. I felt a lot better now that I'd sent it. I hoped that now we could all begin to move forward.

My phone rang, and the display read SCHUYLER W. I answered immediately. "Hey, Shy," I said.

"Omg, Mad!" Schuyler cried. "Are you okay? I just heard from Connor. I can't believe it! Ruth? I mean, *Ruth*? I'm shocked!"

"I know," I said as I stared out at the ducks. "I couldn't believe it either. But it's what happened."

"Well, I certainly can't be friends with her anymore," Schuyler said after a small pause. "I mean, she told everyone about my nose job."

"Sailing accident," I reminded her.

"Right," she said with a laugh. "But I just can't get my head around it! I mean, you two have been BFF since middle school!"

I smiled sadly into the phone. "Elementary, my dear Watson."

******

Twenty minutes later, I was standing on the patio outside of Gofer, holding a cup of hazelnut gelato and a cup of mint chocolate chip, my heart pounding.

I'd called Nate and asked him to meet me there.

This was actually a lot harder than it sounded, because when I started to call him, I realized I didn't have his cell phone number. And I didn't have his parents' house number stored in my cell. So I had to call home and convince Travis to get their number from where my mother had put it on the fridge. Then I had to call Nate's house and ask his mother, who didn't sound that happy to hear from me — I think Nate may have hinted about the whole seeing my ex-boyfriend kissing me thing — but she gave me the number anyway.

And when I finally spoke to Nate, my heart was pounding really, really, hard and I could barely get my words out. He said he was in the middle of running errands, but that he could try and meet up. When he asked where, I completely blanked and suggested the first place I could think of — Gofer.

I looked down at the ice cream in my hands and hoped he would get there soon, as it was starting to melt. But I felt like I couldn't start eating until he arrived. Maybe he wouldn't even hear what I wanted to say to him. Which would be understandable, because as far as he knew, I'd been making out with my ex-boyfriend when he had wanted to *ask me* something.

Maybe he wouldn't believe me. Maybe he didn't even really like me that way, and this had all been in my head. Maybe I'd never find my tortoise, and be like Lonesome George, the famous tortoise in the Galápagos who wandered the sandy beaches alone.

But I just had to make sure he knew the truth.

As I stared out at the parking lot, holding the two cups of rapidly melting ice cream, I saw a red pickup truck pull into the parking lot.

Nate got out and slammed the door. He looked so handsome in his jeans, Cons, and button-down that he literally took my breath away.

Thumpthumpthumpthumpthump, went my heart. I took a tiny bite of gelato for courage as Nate came up the stairs, a black messenger bag slung across his shoulders, and stood next to me — but not too close — at the railing.

"Hey," I said before I lost my nerve entirely and ran away without saying anything because he was just so wonderful and what I was about to do was so scary. I held out the mint chocolate chip to him. "I got this for you. I don't know if you even want it, but I remembered you got it last time, so I thought . . ." I knew I was babbling, but I couldn't seem to stop myself.

"That's great," Nate said. "Thanks." He took his ice cream from me, and then the two of us ate in silence for a few moments.

I seriously had no idea how to begin this. But it felt like the longer I waited, the more it was going to seem like I'd invited him to come silently eat ice cream with me.

"Okay," I said, finally, once we were both almost done with our ice cream. I threw my cup away, even though I still had a few bites left. I just couldn't eat anything else. My stomach was churning, and the butterflies that had been in there at the drive-in had decided to make another appearance. "About the party last night —"

Nate took one last bite, then threw his cup away as well. "Don't worry about it," he said. "I mean, it wasn't like we were there together or anything. Was the guy your ex-boyfriend?"

"Yes," I said. "But it's not —"

"It really doesn't matter to me," he said, looking out at the parking lot. "I mean, you wanted to get back

300

together with him, right? So I'm glad. I'm . . . happy for you."

"No!" I said, hoping with every fiber of my being that he was lying. "It wasn't what it looked like. What you saw last night, I mean."

Nate shook his head. "You mean I didn't see you kissing your ex-boyfriend?" I could hear the hurt in his voice, which made me incredibly happy. He wouldn't sound hurt if he didn't care, right?

"No," I said firmly, "you didn't. You saw my ex-boyfriend kissing *me*. It wasn't like I was kissing him back — or that I'd even wanted to kiss him in the first place."

Nate raised his eyebrows, but he didn't say anything. It seemed like he was listening.

"He wanted to get back together with me," I said, in the interest of full disclosure. "But I don't like him like that. I told him I didn't want to go out with him. Because, um, there's someone else that I like." As I said this, I felt my face get hot, and I had a feeling that it was bright red. I now wished I hadn't thrown out my gelato, just so I could have held it up to my cheeks to cool them off.

Nate looked at me with a small, hopeful smile.

"So," I said, "to make a long story short —"

"Too late," we finished together. His smile got a little wider when I chimed in with him.

301

"Um, I was wondering if you wanted to hang out sometime. I saw that the New Canaan Drive-In is showing *Clue* next weekend, and from everything I've heard, it's a cinematic classic." I looked at Nate for his reaction, but he wasn't saying anything. In fact, he was looking down at the ground, at his messenger bag.

Oh, God.

What if I'd misread this whole thing and he didn't like me at all? What if this was the *third* time this had happened this week? It was possible; I seemed to be misreading signals all over the place. Suddenly, I felt like the world's biggest idiot.

"Or not," I said quickly, my heart not *thump*ing at all, because it was too busy breaking. "That's cool, too. I mean, if you don't want to. I mean . . . that's fine. Never mind."

"Madison," Nate said, with that small, amazing smile of his. He leaned down to his messenger bag and pulled something out. "I just got these developed," he said. He handed me a photo envelope. "Here."

Not really expecting this, I took the envelope and opened it — and saw a picture of myself. I was sitting on the outside deck on the boat in the Galápagos. It was followed by a picture of me smiling at a sea lion, and a picture of me laughing, face turned up to the sun. Then there was a photo of the neon Gofer sign, lit up against the darkening sky and, yes, beautiful. Then there was one of the screen at the drive-in, with lightning bugs darting around, then one of me pointing happily at a tortoise. I looked up at Nate.

"Pictures of me?" I asked, surprised.

"I hope you don't mind," he said. "But it's like I've told you . . . I have a weakness for things that are beautiful."

"Oh," I murmured, not wanting to say anything else, for fear I'd ruin the world's most perfect moment.

He took the photos back from me. "I've been falling for you since the moment I saw you on the boat," he said. "Even though you could clearly never remember my name. So yes, Madison, I'd love to go out with you. It was what I was trying to ask you last night. Just name the day."

"Oh," I said again, my heart beating quickly. "Okay." I smiled at him, and so wide that my cheeks hurt.

"Okay?" he echoed, smiling back at me.

I laughed. "Tewtally."

And then he took a step toward me and I took a step toward him and he reached out and tucked that lock of hair behind my ear, and let his hand linger on my cheek for a moment, and then he leaned down and kissed me.

It was soft at first, his lips just grazing mine. But then it stopped being just a kiss, and became a *kiss*.

Wow.

I seriously don't know how I'd ever thought Justin was a good kisser. Nate was so much better it was like an entirely new thing, and we were kissing and kissing, and it was wonderful, and I was thinking about how glad I was that I'd just had ice cream, because that way I didn't have to worry about my breath at all, and how happy I was we were going to go out that weekend, and *Omg* he was good at the kissing thing.

Then we moved even closer and kept kissing some more, and his hands were in my hair, and I thought about how I was going to see if he wanted to go to the prom with me and probably Stanwich hadn't had their prom yet, and so maybe we could go to two . . .

When I realized that there was lots and lots of time for that.

I knew as soon as I got the chance, I was moving him to the number one spot in my Top 8.

But for right now — and for the foreseeable future — I was happy just to be kissing him.

FRIENDVERSE... *for your galaxy of friends*

Madison
is shopping for prom shoes

Female
16 years old
Putnam, CT
United States

Status: Taken
by Nate

Song: Found My Rosebud/The Thrills
Quote: "Eliminate all other factors, and the one which remains must be the truth." — Sherlock Holmes

Last login: 4/21

TOP 8:

Nate

Shy+Connor

La Feldman

pizzadude

Kittlen

JimmynLiz

ginger_snap

Brian
(grounded)
McMahon

Madison's Blog

Smitten Kitten

We need volunteers for the prom! I swear it has nothing to do with the Titanic!

Buy your Great Dane tickets . . . on sale in the Student Center

Scrabble is the world's most boring game

My brother is not as bad as I'd previously thought

About Me
I'll totally tell you if you have something in your teeth. To your face, not behind your back. Just please return the favor.

General:
Plays, traveling, mysteries, bringing the guilty to justice, pineapple pizza

Music:
Right now, power ballads for the prom DJ

Movies:
Anything at the drive-in

Television:
Currently obsessed with The Hills (thanks a lot, Kittson)

Books:
P.G. Wodehouse, Agatha Christie, Arthur Conan Doyle, SAT prep workbooks

Education: High school
Graduated: Next year . . .

Madison's Comments

Shy+Connor
Mad! Are you and Nate coming in our limo? We need a headcount by tonight! Want to get coffee later??

La Feldman
I'm only going in the limo if Shy promises to cool it with the making out. She and Connor are ridicule!! Non?

pizzadude
Mad, great news — Big Tony threw his back out! I see a pineapple pizza coming your way . . .

Kittlen
Madison, I need your help with the programs! Glen can't do the eyelets as well as you can. And don't forget to bring the glitter to tonight's meeting. And did you hear my mom caught Olivia and Travis making out??!

the8rgrrl
Let's do a line-through tomorrow. Are you free?

ginger_snap
Thanx for the ride home last night, Mad! I have GOT to lay off the O'Douls!

Brian (grounded) McMahon
It was awesome of you and Nate to come and hang out with me yesterday! I think one of these days I might be allowed out of the house again . . .

RueRue
From what I've heard, I think Dell is adjusting to boarding school nicely, though there have been rumors that he's started some sort of gambling ring up there. It's good to be back at school — even though it was only two weeks, it felt longer. Hope all is good with you.

JimmynLiz
Hey Mad, how's it going? You and Nate want to double this weekend?

JimmynLiz
That was both of us. ;)

Nate
I love my tortoise, and I want to thank you properly. Meet you at Gofer in 20 minutes? I'm buying the gelato.

Madison logged out
4/21 3:45 P.M.

"You. Are out of your mind."

My locker door clangs shut with a metallic clanking sound, and for a second Shelby almost looks like she feels bad for sneaking up on me.

Almost.

"Hey, Shelby. Love your jeans—are they new?" I decide to ignore her comment and go straight for the girl talk. I think the jeans are Miss Sixty. They're really cute, with whiskered thighs and full, wide legs.

She leans against my locker and shakes her head at me, her lips pursed tightly. "Flattery will get you nowhere. Don't try to change the subject."

"Are you having PMS?" Zoe chimes in, peeking her head just over Shelby's shoulder. They're like the angel and the devil sitting on my shoulder, whispering in my ears. Except I'm not sure which is which. They seem to be ganging up on me. This is headed nowhere good, and fast.

"Well—no," I stammer. "But I hate it when people blame problems on *that*."

"So this is a new-wave feminist thing you've got going," Z says, puckering her mouth up at the taste of the word *feminist*.

I roll my eyes. "Right. Girls aren't supposed to be student council presidents." I wave a sheet of paper in their direction. "But I've got six signatures here that say otherwise."

"So you're really going through with this?" Zoe asks, looking increasingly grossed out.

I nod. Her reaction is only fueling my fire. "Absolutely. Logan's gotten cocky. He needs to know that he's not the only one who can lead the student body."

"It's social suicide," Zoe says, cracking down hard on a piece of gum.

I glance at Shelby. So far, she seems like the one more likely to be sympathetic. But the look in her eyes says that she's riding the same train as Zoe, and that both of them are seriously convinced I'm headed for self-destructionville.

For the second time in as many days, I falter. Ugh. "You'll . . . vote for me, won't you?"

The back of my throat feels scratchy and hot. It's not possible that my girls would abandon me right now, is it?

To Do List: Read all the *Point* books!

By Aimee Friedman
- [ ] South Beach
- [ ] French Kiss
- [ ] Hollywood Hills
- [ ] The Year My Sister Got Lucky

- [ ] **Airhead** by Meg Cabot

- [ ] **Suite Scarlett** by Maureen Johnson

- [ ] **Love in the Corner Pocket** by Marlene Perez

- [ ] **This Book Isn't Fat, It's Fabulous** by Nina Beck

Hotlanta series by Denene Millner and Mitzi Miller
- [ ] Hotlanta
- [ ] If Only You Knew

- [ ] **Top 8** by Katie Finn

- [ ] **Popular Vote** by Micol Ostow

By Pamela Wells
- [ ] The Heartbreakers
- [ ] The Crushes

Summer Boys series by Hailey Abbott
- [ ] Summer Boys
- [ ] Next Summer
- [ ] After Summer
- [ ] Last Summer

- [ ] **Orange Is the New Pink** by Nina Malkin

Making a Splash series by Jade Parker
- [ ] Robyn
- [ ] Caitlin
- [ ] Whitney